As they came up on the stallion's compound, Darby watched Kanaka Luna's running shape. His dark mane and tail carried on the breeze like gun smoke.

To the left, in the Flatlands, mares and foals drifted toward Pearl pasture. They were reverting to wild instincts, fleeing danger instead of facing it.

So it was kind of weird, Darby thought, that Tango and Hoku, the only two horses that had actually been wild, didn't run.

Darby let out the breath she'd been holding. It made no sense, but she'd been certain the trespasser meant to steal Hoku.

Check out the

Phantom Stallion

series, also by Terri Farley!

Phantom Stallion

WILD HORSE ISLAND 10

FARAWAY FILLY

TERRI FARLEY

HarperTrophy®
An Imprint of HarperCollinsPublishers

Harper Trophy® is a registered trademark
of HarperCollins Publishers.

Faraway Filly

Copyright © 2009 by Terri Sprenger-Farley

All rights reserved. Printed in the United States of America. No part of this book may
be used or reproduced in any manner whatsoever without written permission except in
the case of brief quotations embodied in critical articles and reviews. For information
address HarperCollins Children's Books, a division of HarperCollins Publishers,
1350 Avenue of the Americas, New York, NY 10019.
www.harpercollinschildrens.com

Library of Congress catalog card number: 2008923053
ISBN 978-0-06-162644-9

❖

First Harper Trophy edition, 2009

10
FARAWAY FILLY

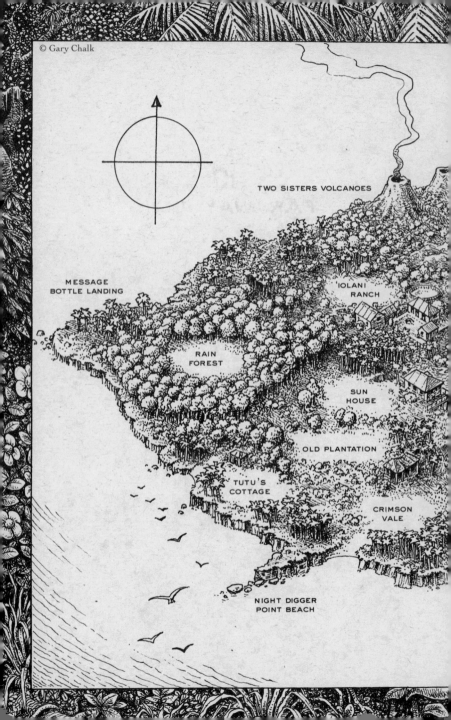

© Gary Chalk

TWO SISTERS VOLCANOES

MESSAGE
BOTTLE LANDING

IOLANI
RANCH

RAIN
FOREST

SUN
HOUSE

OLD PLANTATION

TUTU'S
COTTAGE

CRIMSON
VALE

NIGHT DIGGER
POINT BEACH

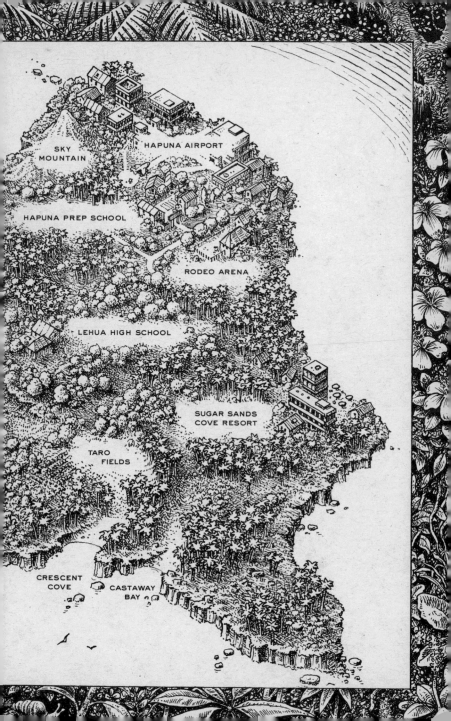

 Chapter One

"Wake up, Darby Leilani."

A voice in the middle of the night was usually scary, but this one wasn't.

Blinking, Darby struggled up on her elbows and looked into her grandfather's face. His white robe hung over his shoulders. He squatted next to her bed.

"It's bright in here," Darby said.

"Horse thief moon, they call it," Jonah told her. "Don't want to scare you, but we've got one."

Did her heart understand his words before her head? Darby's chest filled with thudding.

Don't want to scare you.

That was frightening enough, but *horse thief*!

Those two words made her bolt up and swing her legs off the bed.

"Hoku!" Darby said.

Her grandfather made a disgusted sound as if no horse thief would want her mustang filly when there was a pasture of Quarter Horses to choose from. But he didn't say that.

"Go get Cade. That boy can see in the dark better than I can."

"Okay—"

"I don't just want to scare that thief away. I want to know who he is."

Owl eyes, her friend Megan called Cade, and though there was nothing supernatural about the young paniolo's ability to see in the dark, it was pretty amazing.

"Tell him, take the new ATV, the big one." Jonah made sure Darby nodded before he went on.

"I'm awake," she assured him.

"Tell Cade not to confront rustlers, yeah? Herd the horses away from the crook. Get a license number. That's it."

Darby's brain spun as Jonah left her room.

Just let some stranger try to put a halter on Hoku, Darby thought as she tugged on her jeans. Her wild filly would leave the guy spinning.

She grabbed a T-shirt and pulled it on.

Getting the license number would be tough, but she and Cade could tiptoe up behind the truck and—

"Tell Cade to be careful of the yearlings up in

Two Sisters," Jonah called from the hallway as Darby searched for socks in her dark room. "Don't want them colliding with each other or running into fences. Their brains haven't come in yet and they'll be *pupule* as—what are you waiting for?"

Forget the socks. Darby bolted through her doorway, down the hall, and plopped on the bench by the front door. A row of shoes—from slippers to riding boots—were lined up there.

As Darby worked her bare feet into boots, Jonah opened the front door. The smell of wet grass came in along with a curious *woof* from the dog run.

Darby was on her feet, eyes focused in the direction of the bunkhouse, when Jonah's hand closed on her shoulder.

"Tell Kit to meet me at my truck. We'll take the road and cut 'em off while Cade comes up from the pasture."

Darby nodded once more, then burst into the June night. Overhead, the sky looked like navy blue velvet, on which someone had dropped a new dime.

Full moon. Horse thief moon.

To her right, the cremello horses moved across their pasture like a ghost herd. To her left, the bunkhouse windows were dark, but moonlight made its roof look like wet silver.

What time was it, anyway? The witching hour, she thought. Was that midnight or just sometime really late?

As she jogged, she decided maybe it was dark-thirty. Once when she'd been little and her father had caught her reading in bed before sunrise, he'd told her to go back to sleep because it wasn't even dark-thirty yet.

She'd read that most people died between midnight and four. Was that because everyone else was sound asleep? Was that what the rustler was counting on? Well, he'd picked the wrong ranch.

She'd nearly reached the bunkhouse when she heard the dogs panting with excitement, wondering what she was doing.

"It's okay," Darby called to them, and when she glanced back, the bunkhouse lights were on.

The bunkhouse door stood open. Both Cade and Kit were dressed but hatless and still hopping around, putting on boots.

"Jonah says we have a horse thief," Darby managed. Short of breath, she pointed vaguely toward the pastures. "We're supposed to take the ATV down and spook the horses into running away from him—the bad guy—and he—Jonah—will meet you"—she pointed at Kit—"at the truck."

Her feet had tried to keep up with the pace of her thoughts. Darby leaned forward a little, palms on her thighs, and tried to catch her breath.

Cade came onto the porch and before she could tell him she was fine, she saw he was staring away from her, over the dark pasture. Kit followed and stood, hands on hips, waiting.

No coddling, Darby thought. Unlike her mother, cowboys didn't make a fuss over her oxygen deprivation. Living on a ranch meant asking for help if you needed it. Right now, she didn't.

But Hoku might.

"Do you see anything?" Darby demanded.

Cade shook his head. "The guy must be good."

Darby realized none of them had questioned Jonah's warning. Whatever he'd heard or sensed, they believed him.

Her grandfather had been born on 'Iolani Ranch, just like many Kealohas before him. He knew the sounds and smells belonging to every minute of the day and night. If his instincts said the full moon was lighting the way of a horse thief, he was right.

Cade grabbed a flashlight from inside and hustled toward the newer and quieter of the two ATVs. Darby waited for him to get on, then threw a leg over the vehicle and crowded on behind him.

"Hey," he objected.

"If Jonah didn't want me to go, he would have told me to stay put and call the police or something. Instead, he sent me down here." Darby wasn't certain she was right, but Cade didn't waste time arguing.

Darby took the flashlight he slapped into her palm. Before Cade switched on the key, Kit handed her a cell phone as he jogged past.

How was she supposed to hang on? Hugging her legs to this thing like she would on a horse might not work.

"Hurry," Darby urged Cade, "before I have to carry something else."

But she really had another reason for making Cade hurry. She saw Jonah's outline near his truck. His hands were on his hips. Even though she couldn't make out his features, she'd bet he was glaring her way.

She gave Cade a push with the hand holding the cell phone.

"When did you get so—?"

"He could be after Hoku!" she snapped. "Go!"

They roared into motion, setting off a chorus of barks. As they zipped past the truck, Jonah shouted, "Stop!"

Cade couldn't have heard, because he kept going, concentrating on driving.

The distraction of Megan rushing out of her upstairs apartment, calling, " I wanna go!" was probably to blame for Cade hitting the rock instead of going around it. They stayed airborne for a few seconds before they touched down, banked right, and then sped down the path to the pastures.

"Give me a horse any day," Cade grumbled.

"That's for sure," Darby answered. A horse didn't want to crash on a steep dirt trail. A machine didn't care.

Although moonlight showed the way, Darby felt disoriented for a minute.

Keeping her eyes open while she yawned, Darby

saw they'd taken the trail that ended at Borderlands, the pasture for the saddle herd. At the approach of the snarling ATV, the horses scattered, mostly in groups.

As they came up on the stallion's compound, Darby watched Kanaka Luna's running shape. His dark mane and tail were carried on the breeze like gun smoke.

To the left, in the Flatlands, mares and foals drifted toward Pearl pasture. They weren't moving in a panicky run, but they were reverting to wild instincts, fleeing danger instead of facing it.

So it was kind of weird, Darby thought, that Tango and Hoku, the only two horses that had actually been wild, didn't run.

Darby let out the breath she'd been holding. It made no sense, but she'd been certain the trespasser meant to steal Hoku. Even when she saw her half-wild filly standing so close to Tango that she could have been the rose roan's shadow, Darby wasn't convinced otherwise. Something told her Hoku was the thief's target.

She fought back the urge to call her filly to her. She longed to do it, but lately Hoku had been playing keep-away, and it was pretty embarrassing to be snubbed by your own horse.

Suddenly, though, Darby knew where the intruder was hiding. The horses were telling her.

Trembling and alert, Hoku and Tango stood tall with their ears cast toward Two Sisters pasture, on the slopes leading up to the twin volcanoes.

Was the horse thief moving among the one- and two-year-olds, using them as shields against discovery?

"Jonah said to be careful of the yearlings." She said it so close to Cade's ear, he pulled back and shivered. "He said they'd be crazy."

Cade throttled back the ATV, but he'd probably already known that it would take an experienced hand to catch the young horses. Even Jonah had trouble approaching them. He allowed them to live almost wild, letting them learn to care for themselves as he watched them for traits like speed and intelligence, or weaknesses like aggression and shyness. Their freedom lasted until they were two-year-olds.

"Do you see anything?" Darby asked as the ATV idled. Now that its engine made more of a loud purr, Darby's ears rang with the reverberation of its earlier roar.

Cade didn't answer. He just shook his head.

Tango and Hoku drifted closer to the fence. Across from them, Kanaka Luna moved a few steps uphill. A breeze rushed down from Two Sisters pasture, sending their manes and tails streaming as they kept watch.

Their heads bobbed as they tracked movements. Of what?

There's nothing there, Darby thought. *Nothing but two used-to-be-wild horses, watching the wind dance.*

Chapter Two

"What if there's something there?" Darby asked.

"They smell something, maybe." Cade's tone said he was humoring her as he drove along the fence line. He drove so slowly that the ATV kept lurching forward, but no boards were down, and no posts sagged. Darby didn't catch the fruited meat smell of wild pigs, or the snarling chaos of feral dogs.

Darby tried to picture what the horses sensed. There were two gates on the northwest side of the high pasture, next to the dirt road farthest from Sun House.

As she watched, the shape of the ranch truck materialized, up on the road that bordered the Two Sisters pasture. After a while its headlights flashed, telling

Darby and Cade they could go on home.

"I don't know how a rustler would arrange to steal a horse here," Cade muttered.

"Wouldn't it be easier and more profitable to steal cattle?" Darby reasoned. "They could be noisy, but one is just about as good as another and they could be sold before they were identified by brands or ear marks."

Cade didn't seem to even hear her cattle rustler proposition. He was more interested in puzzling out how someone would rob 'Iolani Ranch of horses.

"He coulda come on foot," Cade speculated, "if he only meant to catch one or two horses and lead them out." But he wasn't satisfied with that idea. "Anyone who knows ranch horses would know they'd have to take their time and not spook them."

Darby agreed. She'd only lived on a ranch for a few months and she knew horses that ran loose would be trickier to catch than those kept in stalls.

"If you were smart, you woulda already scoped them out," Cade said. "Picked out the valuable ones."

"But then, if you came back in the dark," Darby said, "wouldn't they all look pretty much the same? It would be too risky to mark them. And if they started acting up . . ."

"He could come on horseback," Cade suggested, "but that wouldn't make for a quick getaway and he'd risk being seen, ponyin' someone else's horse on down the road."

They sat in silence for a minute. Then Darby said, "I'd bring a stock truck with a ramp."

"Or at least a horse trailer," Cade agreed. Then he gave a frustrated sigh and shifted in his seat, scanning the hills and ridges around them. "For now, it would help if I knew what Jonah heard or saw."

Or felt, Darby thought.

Since Tango and Hoku had returned to grazing and the truck had flashed them an all-clear sign, Cade turned away from Two Sisters and drove across the broodmares' enclosure, toward Pearl pasture.

"Blue Moon looks fine," she whispered to Cade. The foal was excited, kicking up his heels, thinking this was a game, although he had been terribly sick with colic just last week.

Cade nodded, then stopped the ATV at the fence. The night was so silent, they heard wind passing through an owl's wings as it swooped overhead.

As if the owl had signaled him that it was safe to come out of hiding, a palomino named Doubloon emerged amid a sudden leafy rustling. He was followed by a troop of horses, including Baxter, a blue roan cow pony Darby had ridden in a recent rodeo.

She was just about to coax Baxter closer when the sound of an engine and the squeal of tires made Darby look back at the upper pasture.

"Bet they were laid up, hiding," Cade said.

"And then when Kit and Jonah drove past, they took off," Darby guessed.

Cade stared into the darkness. "Need some binoculars."

Even though they couldn't see what was happening, this was getting exciting, Darby thought.

What if Kit and Jonah intercepted the bad guys? Neither man was violent, but they were devoted to the ranch and its horses. Would they be able to hold their tempers?

At last, the cell phone vibrated in Darby's hand. Kit was talking before she said hello.

"Took off on us," Kit said. "You two go on back to the ranch. Get some sleep."

"Okay," Darby said, but by the time they reached the ranch yard, Cade had decided to wait up for Jonah and Kit. After all, it was nearly four o'clock.

Darby smothered another yawn. Four o'clock sounded more like night than morning. And who knew when Jonah and Kit would return?

It was too early to do chores. And last night Aunty Cathy had been busy making a monster "to do" list that she'd warned the girls would be tacked on the office wall at seven A.M. sharp.

It didn't take long for weariness to win out over curiosity. With three more hours of sleep, she told herself, she'd be better prepared to face whatever happened. Darby gave in and crawled back into bed.

Munching on a green apple, Darby strolled into the ranch office at seven o'clock and stopped short.

"Hi," she said, surprised that Megan, Aunty Cathy, and Jonah were already there.

Megan looked like she usually did at the start of a soccer match. Cherry-Coke-colored hair fell over her shoulder, and her body braced in anticipation, but she still gave Darby a smile and wave as she listened to Jonah's account of the night before.

". . . no one there, but the loop, you know? That goes over the gatepost? Not on right. Not double-twisted, just flopped over . . ."

Most of the gates on 'Iolani Ranch closed with bolts and latches. In a few of the higher pastures, extra gates were made of rope and sturdy branches, but everyone was instructed in how to close them securely.

Everyone but the horse thief, she thought.

"Any yearling could've nudged it open," Jonah said.

"It's a good thing you got up there right away," Aunty Cathy told him. "Or we would have been chasing horses all over the island."

Megan leaned back against the office desk, and sighed at this unexciting end to the story.

"Were there tire tracks or anything in the dirt?" Megan prodded.

"Couldn't tell in the dark, but Kit's back up there now," Jonah said.

"I don't get it," Megan said. "Not to be rude, but why did you think it was a person up there? Maybe some wild bull was up there."

"You been seein' wild bulls around, Mekana?" Jonah teased. He actually looked pleased at Megan's challenge. "Here's the thing," Jonah continued, sketching each scene in the air with his gestures. "We were driving back home, yeah? Kit catches a flash in the rearview mirror." Jonah lowered his voice and leaned toward Megan. "We look back over our shoulders, like this? And see a car creeping down the road opposite of the way we're going, *with its lights out*!"

"Not normal," Darby blurted. She wasn't enjoying Jonah's tale. That ominous feeling from last night, the fear that someone was about to steal Hoku, was back.

"By the time Kit swung the truck around, that trespasser drove off into the woods, goin' toward"—he gestured vaguely—"the whatchacallits' place."

"The Zinks," Darby supplied, and when Jonah just nodded, she asked, "So what happened next?"

Jonah shrugged. "We came home."

"Probably it was nothing more than an adventurous tourist." Aunty Cathy sounded as if that was routine. "This time of year, it's what makes the most sense."

"Going into our pastures in the middle of the night?" Darby asked. "And driving around with their lights out?"

"No one wants to hurt our horses," Megan said, knowing right away that her friend was more worried about Hoku than safe driving.

Worried and fidgety, Darby wondered what Jonah was thinking. His expression told her nothing and he wouldn't let her catch his eyes.

"Got salt licks to replace, if you *wahines* will excuse me," he said.

Jonah left and Darby followed, unsure what to say. Before anything came to her, Navigator, the big coffee-black gelding with rusty rings around his eyes, blocked her way.

"Hi, boy," she said. "Move."

Navigator backed away from her flailing hand, but he kept pace with Darby, extending his brownish lips for her apple core.

Since she still wasn't sure how to explain her uneasiness to Jonah, Darby stopped. Her grandfather clearly didn't want to be caught. His horseman's stride, stiff but graceful, was taking him quickly out of range.

Blinking with sympathy, Navigator approached again.

"Here you go," Darby said, feeding the core to him.

Then, since she still hadn't checked Aunty Cathy's list, she returned to the ranch office.

"Just let me get this open and you can help me," Megan said as Darby stepped inside.

Megan knelt beside one of the large boxes that had arrived the day before. She fought to peel back a strip of tenacious tape while Aunty Cathy worked at the computer.

As she waited for Megan to win the battle, Darby

glanced over Aunty Cathy's shoulder. It looked like she was designing forms for use in their new guest rider program.

Aunt Babe's Sugar Sands Cove Resort would supply most of the guests, but the appearance of Cash, the cremello, in the *keiki* rodeo had sparked interest from a Girl Scout troop and individual riders, too.

"One will be a checklist for us to use when they call," Aunty Cathy explained, as her fingers pecked at the keyboard. "I think most of them will phone ahead to make reservations for a ride, don't you? Or Babe's staff will call. The one I type up next will be for them to fill in on arrival."

How many in your party? What are their ability levels? One- or two-hour ride? Darby read. Then, she skipped to two underlined statements: *Wear boots or shoes with a heel. No children under eight. Wear helmet or sign waiver.*

"What's a waiver, exactly?" Darby asked.

"It's something you sign, saying you don't have the good sense to wear a helmet," Aunty Cathy said. "Our insurance company requires it."

"Ta da!" Megan sang a fanfare as the box popped open to expose the riding helmets inside.

"What color are they?" Aunty Cathy asked. "I got a deal if I accepted the suppliers' color choice."

"Burnt sienna," Megan read from the invoice she'd taken out of the box.

While she held up one of the reddish brown helmets for her mother's approval, Darby attacked the next box.

It held a second bargain, this one courtesy of Cricket, the feed store manager.

"These are great," Darby said, taking nylon "rope" halters in brown and gold from the box. "Why did she get a discount on them?"

"They're last year's colors." Aunty Cathy pushed away from the computer and examined one of the gold halters. "What do you think?" she asked the girls.

"Jonah will think they're too flashy," Darby said.

"No, they'll look great on white horses," Megan countered.

"And they were practically free," Aunty Cathy said. "I'd say we did pretty good for shopping the bargains."

Aunty Cathy had been talking almost nonstop about money, and the upkeep cost of the "free" cremello horses. Even though she'd led the campaign to convince Jonah they needed another source of income besides the sale of Quarter Horses and beef, Aunty Cathy was worried about the cost of launching the guest rider program.

So far, they only had one scheduled ride. The Girl Scout troop was arriving tomorrow afternoon, and Darby was sure that was why Aunty Cathy's plans and preparations had accelerated. Everything had to be perfect for the first ride so the program would get a good review and more people would come. Which meant there was a ton of work to be done today.

Still, Aunty Cathy could see past the hassle. She

and Megan discussed how great it would be when Megan could work the phones and register riders, and Aunty Cathy could get out of the office and enjoy the beautiful place in which she lived.

"And we should all know the mounts well enough that we can match horses with riders," Aunty Cathy said as she pointed to the chore list on the office wall.

Darby was just admitting to herself that she didn't know all the cremellos' names, when she saw the chore list would remedy that problem.

Darby
1) Keep three cremellos groomed, healthy, and beautiful

A glance at Megan's list showed her that Megan was responsible for the other three.

2) Saddle "your" three horses each day they have riders and check them over after they're back and return them to pasture
3) Be the backup guide for trail rides

Another look at the lists next to hers showed Darby that Megan and Aunty Cathy were alternating with each other and Kimo as head guides.

4) Feed Pigolo, Francie, dogs
5) Clean up after Pigolo, Francie, dogs

She was already doing those things.

6) *Halter break Inkspot and Luna Dancer*

Inky was a wild colt from Black Lava's herd and Luna Dancer was a purebred Quarter Horse colt from the ranch. Darby wasn't sure if the weanlings were getting wilder while they shared a corral with Medusa, Kit's wild steeldust mare, but she hoped not.

"I've never trained a horse to halter," Darby admitted. "In fact, I've never trained a horse."

"Of course you have, sis." Megan jiggled Darby's shoulder as if she were shaking some sense into her. "What about Hoku?"

"That's been more like making friends, or something," Darby said.

"That 'or something' is training," Aunty Cathy assured her.

Darby wasn't so sure about that, but she didn't have time to sink into a bad mood over Hoku's recent aloofness.

"Look at the clock!" Aunty Cathy said. "Where's Cade?"

"Ma'am?" As Cade spoke from the doorway, they all jumped.

"You do that on purpose," Megan accused Cade.

He shrugged, but Darby saw his amusement. Usually he acted more mature than fifteen, but every now and then Cade did something like that, which reminded her he was only two years older than she was.

He shifted his weight from one boot to the other, then touched his lau hala hat brim. If he stepped inside, he'd have to remove his hat, so he stayed in the doorway and looked at Darby. "Ready?"

"For what?" Darby asked.

From somewhere outside, there came the sound of hammering.

Darby turned to Megan. Her friend shrugged and then Aunty Cathy looked up from her work.

"I forgot to tell you," Aunty Cathy said. "Well, ask you, really, but could you drive into Hapuna with Cade and pick up the saddles and bridles we're buying—used—from the hotel there? They give rides on the beach and they're replacing their gear this season."

"Sure," Darby said.

"I'll get the truck."

Darby watched Cade go, and though she was glad to visit a new place and be the first to see the new tack, she didn't really think he'd need her along to help load it up.

Aunty Cathy saw her confusion. "Mudge, the barn boss, is a little tough to get along with. Jonah says he's shifty, but I think he's just unhappy we're starting a competing business."

Darby could tell Aunty Cathy was being generous to Mudge. It sounded like a made-up name, but what did Jonah mean by shifty? Dishonest?

"He did brighten up a bit when I offered to buy the hotel's used horse gear," Aunty Cathy continued. "Cade will make sure it's just well broken in—"

"Not thrashed," Megan clarified.

"—while you establish a business relationship," Aunty Cathy said, "since you're a good talker."

"Like she really sweet-talked Mr. Klaus," Megan teased.

Darby blushed. "I was under undue stress."

Darby wished Megan hadn't brought it up, but it was a mistake she should remember and learn from. Arguing with the state official who'd proposed herding wild horses with a helicopter had nearly backfired.

"It turned out all right in the end," Megan assured her.

"And from now on I'm doing what Kit said."

"Listening twice as much as you talk, since you were born with two ears and one mouth," Megan recited in a singsong voice.

"Sort of," Darby said. "Did you get that advice, too?"

"Not from him." Megan slid a glance toward her mother.

"You'll do fine. Better than Jonah, certainly," Aunty Cathy said.

"Or Cade," Megan said. "He's just too shy. I wish I could go, but Mom wants to teach me all this office stuff."

At the sound of an approaching vehicle, Aunty Cathy stood.

"Here comes Cade." Aunty Cathy walked outside and opened the passenger-side truck door for Darby. She leaned partway inside, giving Cade advice, too. "If we expect the horses to carry riders for hours, several times each week, the saddles have to fit . . ." Aunty Cathy's voice trailed off, as if she'd thought of something else, but then she shook her head and smiled. "There's so much to do, but by the time you get back, Megan will have each of the cremellos fitted with a new halter—"

"That's not on my list," Megan protested, but her mother's harried expression made Megan add, "Of course, I'll be glad to do it."

". . . and that will make fitting the saddles and bridles easier and then we'll hang them all on hooks in the tack room—oh, I'd better tell Kimo to put them up, and each hook should be labeled with the horse's name to save time in the morning when we tack up . . ."

Aunty Cathy strode back into the office, but she reemerged before the girls could say anything. Jotting on a clipboard as she walked toward the hammering, she said, "This is going to be a busy day for all of us."

"Yes, ma'am," Cade said.

Darby closed her door and looked at Megan. Neither of them rolled their eyes or felt put-upon.

"We've got it made," Darby whispered. "Working with horses all summer."

"Arranging the rides and meeting new people—"

"See what you think by the end of summer," Cade put in.

Megan laughed. "Doesn't he sound just like Jonah?"

They'd driven out of the ranch yard, down the dirt road, and crossed the cattle guard when Darby realized she was humming.

They sped down the street, flanked on both sides with trees and endless green fields. Then, since they were far enough away that she was out of danger of being asked to help, Darby asked, "What was all that hammering?"

"Kit replacing a board on Hoku's corral," Cade said.

Cade kept his eyes on the road and Darby didn't say a word, but her contentment crashed as she thought about her displaced horse.

Her wild sorrel filly had stood by her through earthquakes, a volcanic eruption, and a tsunami, but she couldn't tolerate neglect. *That's how it must feel to her,* Darby thought. Hoku couldn't understand Darby had been overwhelmed lately with school, the rodeo, a sick pony, Black Lava and his herd, Patrick Zink, and Mistwalker.

But I love her, Darby thought, *and that's what counts.*

Luckily, her "summer job" would keep her on the ranch near Hoku. She'd pounce on every chance to show her filly just how much she loved her.

That would be a lot easier if Hoku hadn't been evicted from her home corral by Medusa, but she couldn't blame Kit for wanting a horse of his own. Or for choosing a wild one.

Medusa, Kit's beautiful steeldust, had a lead mare's attitude and a fierce spirit like Hoku's. But Kit and Medusa had made progress since Inkspot, a foal from Medusa's old herd, had come to 'Iolani Ranch.

Yesterday, the mare had calmed down enough that Kit had been able to touch a brush to her tangled mane.

"Last night Medusa kicked a board pretty good," Cade said. "Didn't break it, just loosened the nails, but Kit's afraid she mighta weakened it, and he wants everything right for when Hoku moves back in."

Kit was such a good guy, Darby thought. He'd worked on the broken fence after spending most of the night searching for a horse thief.

"So, did Kit tell you anything else about the rustler?" Darby asked. "Jonah didn't have much to say."

"Whoever opened the gate was an average-sized man with average-sized feet," Cade said.

"Where did Mr. Average go after he opened the gate?" Darby kept her voice as light as she could, but she didn't feel that way.

"He walked far enough into the pasture that he woulda been able to see Sun House."

"That's not—" Darby didn't know how to finish what she'd started. Prowlers belonged in the city, not here. From the day she'd stepped onto 'Iolani Ranch, it had offered her a sense of sanctuary. She knew that sounded kind of dramatic, but that's how she felt.

"Might be someone from outta town. Had jet lag and stopped to look around."

They both heard the lameness of his suggestion, so Darby didn't argue that, jet-lagged or not, a man would've already had a loose grasp on right and wrong if he went for a midnight stroll on private property.

"I'm not scared. It's just that no one has the right to—" Darby searched for the right word, but it wouldn't come to her. "Intrude? Trespass? Invade our privacy? You know."

"I do," Cade said. "Spent years thinking Manny would miss hammering on me and sneak onto the ranch to catch up."

He said it in an off-handed way, as if beatings and visions of his stepfather coming after him in the dark were as much a part of his childhood as Dee's home-baked cookies.

"Jonah would never allow that," Darby said, but she knew it wasn't enough, even though Cade just shrugged.

"Just jokin'," he said.

Darby didn't believe that, but she tried to respond with a dark joke of her own.

"If there'd been a jail break, I think we would've heard," Darby said.

And Cade smiled.

 Chapter Three

The Royal Hapuna Hotel was more spread out and showy than Aunt Babe's Sugar Sands Cove resort. Instead of pure white, the hotel's buildings were pink and purple and their logo—shown on the shirts of all employees—seemed to be a shaka-wielding gecko.

After a few minutes of aimless wandering, Darby asked a uniformed employee where they could find the stable. He told them to follow the orchid-colored fence past the swimming pool, snack bar, and riding ring and they'd find it.

"Orchid fence," Cade muttered as he and Darby strode between manicured flower beds.

They'd passed the snack bar and pool, and the whitewashed stable was in sight when Darby noticed a man standing by a paddock. It wasn't the purple fence that made her take a second look. It was the man.

Something about him caught Darby's eye. He was smoking a cigarette, which set him apart from most of the tourists around him, but that wasn't it. He looked more Native American than Hawaiian. When he'd been younger, he might've had Kit's good looks. But the years seemed to have shaped his mouth into a permanent sneer.

Do I know him? Darby wondered as they walked on. It was possible. After all, people from around the world came to Hawaii on vacation.

Staying in step with Cade, Darby glanced over her shoulder.

And caught the man looking back at her.

Darby jerked her gaze away and aimed her eyes straight ahead until the stable was right in front of them. Three glossy horses, tied to a long hitching rail, dozed in the sun. All three had tails docked straight across the bottoms.

Probably right where their tailbones ended, Darby speculated. Their gleaming necks were bare because their manes were shaved into little Mohawks.

"Low-maintenance grooming," Cade said.

Darby weighed convenience against beauty for a second. As they entered an air-conditioned office adjoining the long stable, she braced herself for the "tough-to-get-along-with" Mudge.

A man in a hotel staff uniform sat at a desk. Before

she could read his name tag, she knew this was not the grumpy barn boss. But Darby wasn't sure how else to open their conversation, so she said, "We're looking for Mr. Mudge."

This man looked up with a welcoming smile and Darby saw his name tag read "Richard."

"I'm afraid you missed him. He quit work two days ago. I'm just the interim manager, but I'll try to help you."

Minutes later, Darby and Cade were relieved to learn that Mudge had left the gear and paperwork for 'Iolani Ranch. They walked out to a swept concrete pad inside the barn where the tack was stacked. Cade sorted through it, checking stitching and looking for wear, then declared it perfect.

"Thanks, Richard," Darby said, reaching out to shake his hand.

"Ri*ɔ*har*ɔ*." He corrected her pronunciation and accepted her handshake at the same time. "It looks like everything's in order, but I couldn't swear to it. I've been with the hotel for six years, and I've always worked inside, mostly in housekeeping. Maybe that's what confused the staff in Human Resources. *House-keeping, horsekeeping.*"

Darby laughed politely, then said, "I wish I could help."

"Maybe you can," he said, snapping his fingers. "I don't know anything about horses, and this note Mudge left doesn't quite make sense to me."

Cade and Darby went over the stapled pages that documented Mudge's last official act.

"It looks like he hired a cowboy, for room and board only," Darby read. "To work the kinks out of the dude string before the start of the tourist season."

Darby glanced around. Room and board must mean a luxury hotel room and restaurant meals. That was a sweet deal.

"Probably this sounds simple to you," Richard said, tapping the file, "but the *kinks* and *string* part leaves me a bit confused."

Cade managed to explain that it looked as if the cowboy had been hired to put the horses through their paces, and erase any lazy habits they'd developed.

"You're probably right." Richard narrowed his eyes in thought, then shook his head. "I do hope Mr. Stone is better with animals than he is with humans. But what do I know? I'm a little too fastidious for all this dust and poop. It's not my scene at all. *That's* more like it."

He nodded his sleek hair toward the patio dining area, and when Darby looked, she spotted a bus boy she knew from Lehua High School.

Today he was dressed in black pants and a white shirt with a clip-on tie, and his hair was slicked down, but Darby remembered him from the day of the earthquake.

She'd cut in line behind Megan while they waited to buy food from the snack cart. When she'd flashed a sheepish look to the person behind her and asked, "Is it okay?" it had been this guy.

She didn't know his name, but he'd looked half asleep, shoulders hunched, hands shoved deep in the pockets of baggy shorts with hair rumpled into something like a cockatoo's crest. In slow motion, he'd blinked as if she'd wakened him, and waved his hand, telling her to go ahead.

Later, she'd discovered his best buddy was Tyson, Darby's least favorite guy at Lehua High School.

Richard drew Darby's attention back by mentioning that guests were fascinated by the "cowboy."

"In the two days I've been in this job, I've seen them watching him from the patio and gathering around the riding ring, as if the circus had come to town."

"Really?" Darby asked. As the granddaughter of a "horse charmer" maybe this was something she should see.

"If you hurry, you can catch him 'working the kinks out' of a horse now. She's got the cutest name, Jellybean Jewel, but she rolls in the dirt and will *not* be bathed."

Darby glanced at Cade, wondering if he was making the same comparison she was. It had only taken Kit a week to get Medusa to let him touch her mane, and the mare was wild. How hard could it be to train a domesticated horse to allow a bath? Maybe the cowboy was enjoying the perks of his job too much to hurry.

Darby and Cade made a trip to the truck with a

wheeled cart full of saddles. Before Darby could suggest they watch the horse trainer, Cade was already shaking his head.

"We've got time to watch for just a few minutes," Darby insisted as they walked back for the rest of the tack. Darby knew he was thinking of Aunty Cathy's parting words about all the work waiting at the ranch.

They'd returned the cart and slung bridles and reins over their shoulders when they were surprised by a sharp neigh, cut off in mid-utterance.

Richard must have thought Cade's frown was directed at him, because he said, "I can't use her if she looks like a dust bunny, not when guests are paying good money to stay here and be pampered."

They were ready to go as soon as they put the bridles in the truck, but Darby wasn't about to leave without seeing that horse. Its neigh had sounded bewildered.

"Thanks again, Richard," Darby said, shaking the man's hand. "Good luck getting the other job."

"Thanks," he said, and then he pointed out the way to the corral.

"We've gotta get back," Cade said.

Darby might have gone along with him if Cade hadn't dangled the truck keys in front of her eyes.

"You might have the keys, but you're not in charge," she said.

"Then who is?" he asked.

Darby didn't give him the satisfaction of an answer;

she just started walking.

"Dad, come see the polka-dot horse!" A sunburned child in a visor and shorts was tugging his father toward the corral.

Cade was partial to Appaloosas like his gelding, Joker, so it could have been the child's comment, but Darby credited her determination, too, when Cade gave in.

Darby and Cade weren't the only ones standing at the purple fence, waiting to see the cowboy and the Appaloosa.

"Wow, she's gorgeous," Darby said, and Cade nodded.

The kind-eyed Appaloosa mare *was* dirty, as Richard had said, but it wasn't hard to see past the smears and smudges. She had a reddish mane and tail and strawberry markings that looked like someone had flung a handful of jelly beans on her grass-stained white coat.

She stood on one side of the corral, freckled ears pointed at the trainer, but every now and then she glanced down at a bubble-gum-pink hose. Water gushed out of it, forming a puddle on the grass.

As the mare checked out the trainer, so did Darby. He was the man she'd glimpsed before, Darby realized, the one she'd thought was Native American.

Now, she wasn't so sure. His outfit looked like a costume: white cowboy hat, green silk scarf, a denim jacket snapped from his throat to his waist, brown work pants, and scuffed boots. He wore a fanny pack, too, and he was turning its zippered side around to the front and removing a little glass jar.

"At seven years old, she's broke and gentle, but stubborn as a mule," he said in a voice pitched to carry to those who were watching.

"Naw."

Cade's comment was so quiet, Darby asked, "What?"

Cade frowned as the trainer put the glass jar away, then coiled the long rope connected to the mare's halter, pulling her closer.

Eager to meet him, the Appaloosa took three steps forward.

"Mama!" A little girl's voice piped up beside Darby. "That smells like the stuff you put on your knee after you go jogging."

"It does." The woman beside them had boy-short hair and an athletic build. She flashed a self-conscious smile at Darby. "Doesn't it smell like heat rub?"

Darby nodded, then looked at Cade for confirmation. His lips were pressed together in disapproval.

"Why would he—?"

Cade made a keep-your-voice-down motion as the trainer reached the horse.

"It's some kinda menthol," Cade whispered as the trainer caught hold of the cheek strap on the mare's halter.

The man didn't speak to the horse as he applied a

thick sheen of the gel on her delicate nostrils.

"That's gotta sting," the jogger said.

The Appaloosa didn't pull away, even though her head jerked up and her eyes widened in alarm.

"But why's he doing that?" Darby asked. The jogger-mother leaned forward to hear Cade's answer.

"Covers up his smell so she won't recognize it the next time."

Darby sucked in a breath. Why didn't he want her sense of smell to connect him to what happened next?

The burn from the gel must have intensified, because the mare pulled her head away and rolled her eyes at the trainer.

If he understood her reproach, he didn't care.

"Gotta show her humans are in charge, if she's going to behave for your beach rides," the trainer said. "This won't hurt her."

Darby thought *this* was the menthol rub, but the trainer quickly moved to step two.

Maintaining a grip on the lead rope, he tucked in close to the Appaloosa. Then, with a hand so quick Darby wasn't sure what she was seeing, he grabbed her tail. Next, his hands came together and he tied the mare up short to her own tail.

"That's an accident waiting to happen." The comment came from a mustached man who stood holding his suitcase. He seemed unable to look away or keep walking toward the lobby.

"It's no accident," the trainer said. He backed toward

the pink hose. "This is cause and effect, y'know? I'm gonna wash her. What she does is up to her."

Except that she doesn't understand that, Darby thought, *and he hasn't tried to show her what will happen.* Darby knew if she did such a thing to Hoku, she'd buck and fall. Or run in circles until she got dizzy and fell. Without meaning to, Darby found herself holding on to the winged heart charm on her necklace and sawing it back and forth on its chain.

The Appaloosa—Jellybean Jewel, Darby remembered—was trying to understand on her own. Calm but confused, she pulled back, winced at the tug on her tail, then walked forward.

"She's a smart one," Cade said. This time he didn't keep his voice down. When the trainer looked his way, Cade added, "But she doesn't know what you're askin' for."

"She will," the trainer said, too sure of himself to take advice.

He hung his hat on a fence post, raised the silk scarf up to his brow, and knotted it on like a sweatband. Then he stood there, smoked a cigarette, and watched the horse.

The Appaloosa's balance was hard to believe. She increased her speed, trotting in circles like a dog chasing its tail.

A few people laughed. Didn't they know how cruel this was? Some did, Darby thought, because the runner-mother led her child over to a man who must be her father, placed the little girl's hand in his, then jogged away.

Some people just ducked out on problems, Darby thought, but she wouldn't, and she couldn't take her eyes off the Appaloosa, either.

Even in her awkward position, Jellybean Jewel stayed on her feet.

You could do anything with that horse, Darby thought. *Dressage, cutting, search and rescue . . .*

But then the trainer lifted the pink hose. Dizzy on wobbling legs, the mare tried to be submissive. Her head bobbed as she tried to focus on him, but that move pulled her tail. He lifted the hose higher, so that the water's descent into the grass made a splattering sound. Never touching her with the water, he approached from all sides at a run, darting closer each time.

The Appaloosa clamped her tail down in fear. The action jerked her head around.

"I've got to help," Darby said.

Cade's face was red. "Whether it works or not, this is no good."

"I'll go tell Richard," Darby said. He'd allowed the "cowboy" to start this performance. He had to make him stop it.

"Wait," Cade said. He pointed.

The guy she'd recognized from school had come out of the restaurant—on a break, maybe. He ran both hands through his hair and it sprang up.

It was definitely Tyson's friend. His eyes stayed on the horse in the riding ring as he pulled his clip-on tie loose and gripped it so hard it disappeared inside his fist. Then, he threw it down.

The sound of the mare clapping her jaws made Darby turn back. Using the body language of a foal to a fierce stallion, the Appaloosa was saying, "Don't hurt me."

When the trainer ignored the gesture, the mare's ears finally flattened and she lifted a front leg. Anyone could tell she was saying, "I don't want to, but I *will* strike you."

The man—Darby couldn't think of him as a cowboy—put his thumb over the end of the hose and shot a jet of water at the mare's belly.

In an instant, she arched her back, trying to escape the cold water, lunged toward him, then fell.

With a choked neigh, she struggled, but she couldn't rise.

Of course not, Darby thought. *Horses swing their heads and necks for momentum.* The mare tried rolling and kicking and he squirted her again.

That's it, Darby thought, but her feet wouldn't move. She knew what she had to do, but her mind was too close to the mare's. The tendons in her own neck strained. She heard the man's lecturing as an unknown language. Silently, she asked people why they were walking away, abandoning her to this torturer.

And then the water stopped.

"Hey!" The trainer yelled at a guy standing by the faucet. "Turn that back on!"

Tyson's friend wore an expression so puzzled, it had to be fake. He fiddled with the handle. From here it was impossible to tell what he was really doing, but Darby had a feeling it wasn't much. And he was trying to cover up by acting too dumb for sabotage.

"I don't know, sir. This happens alla time here, yeah?" he said, shaking his head.

He wasn't from *here*, he was from Nevada, the trainer muttered. Then he added, "Even in that desert, water comes out of a hose when you turn the handle."

Nevada? The word gave Darby chills, but she didn't have time to wonder why.

A waitress leaned out of the restaurant and called, "Pauli, your break's over. You're going to get fired this time if you don't hurry."

But the kid, Pauli, didn't stop.

"Nev-AH-da," he mused. "Next to Nebraska? North Dakota?" The few hotel guests who were still around laughed, and Pauli shrugged. "All those bogus *N* states got snow, yeah?"

He shuddered in clownish disgust and that was the last straw for the trainer. He flung the pink hose onto the grass and walked away, leaving the horse on her side, taking shallow breaths.

 Chapter Four

Cade and Pauli swarmed over the fence together.

Once he was inside, Pauli hesitated, but Cade edged around behind the horse, squatted on his boot heels, and held a calming hand against the Appaloosa's neck.

"You're fine now," he said quietly, then glanced at Pauli. "Wipe that junk off her nose before I cut the rope."

Pauli tugged his white shirt from the waistband of his trousers and knelt in front of the Appaloosa. At first he dabbed his shirttail at the mare's nostrils. When she didn't react with panic, he leaned over her, wiping her tender nose clean.

As soon as Pauli finished, Cade sawed his pocket

knife through the lead rope. Cade was trying to dis-
entangle the rope from the horse's tail when she slung
her head up. He and Pauli jumped back as the mare's
front hooves dug out tufts of grass and she lurched up
on all fours.

Her brown eyes rolled. She snorted, then stared at
the humans surrounding her.

Cade made a gesture to Pauli. "Let's keep back, let
her walk around and see he's gone."

Go, Darby told herself, and she ran toward the stable office, the last place she'd seen Richard. She wanted
to get there before that awful excuse for a trainer did.

The mother-jogger had beaten her to it.

Darby skidded up to the office as Richard said,
"His contract with the hotel—if he had one—will be
canceled."

The woman's expression was angry and determined. She lifted her chin toward Darby and said,
"She can back me up."

Richard made a smoothing motion. "I believe you.
He didn't strike the right chord with me when I met
him, but he was hired by my predecessor."

"Is there someone else I should report him to, as
well?"

"Not necessary," Richard assured her. "He won't
get his hands on Jellybean Jewel again."

"Okay." The woman looked somewhat satisfied as
she passed Darby.

"Thanks for getting here before me," Darby said.

When the woman grinned and held her hand up for a high five, Darby returned it.

"So, I'm still stuck with a filthy horse," Richard said with a sigh after the woman had left.

"For now," Darby said, "but she's a sweet mare—"

"Except for biting and kicking," he said.

"She didn't even defend herself," Darby said. "She tried to run away." Richard's expression said he wasn't angry, he just felt powerless to correct this problem.

"Do you have time to just walk over with me and see how she's doing?" Richard asked.

If she'd sprinted away from the corral and left some other guy to help the horse, Darby wouldn't have felt so confident, but Cade was there.

Exhausted and confused, the Appaloosa stood in the shade, as far from humans as she could get.

"She'll be okay, won't she?" Richard asked.

"I think so," Darby told him, "but the way he had her head tied to her tail, it would probably be a good idea to have a vet look at her."

"We actually have a vet on-site today," Richard said. "Doctor Luke's here examining one of the geckos in the lobby terrarium. If you can get her into that grassy paddock over there, I'll have him stop by."

"Good," Darby said. Richard took his job seriously, even if it was temporary.

"She's a big sturdy animal," Richard observed.

Just because horses were big didn't mean they

were indestructible, Darby thought. She couldn't help picturing the mare's spine strained like a drawn bow.

"Thanks for your help," Richard said as Cade and Pauli came out of the corral. He extended his hand to shake theirs, but hesitantly.

Cade's short tight braid was unraveling. Pauli's wrinkled shirt smelled like heat rub. They both looked a little sweaty and a lot pleased with themselves.

"That's okay," Cade said, and gave Richard's hand a quick shake.

"Pauli Akua," the other boy said, pointing to his name tag. "And I should get back to work, but I'm still kind of amped."

Darby couldn't be sure, but she thought he meant *excited* from rescuing Jewel.

The man with the suitcase still stood nearby. Recognizing Richard as a hotel staffer, he said, "I don't know where these young men learned to handle horses, but they were amazing."

Eyebrows raised, Richard turned to Cade for an explanation.

"I work on 'Iolani Ranch."

"He's a paniolo," Darby said. "A Hawaiian cowboy, sort of, except they were roping cattle out in the rain forests for a long time before the mainland cowboys."

"Awesome," Pauli said.

"Really?" Richard and the guest said at the same time.

They looked fascinated, Darby thought.

She didn't mean to brag, but she smiled as she added, "There are generations of paniolos in my family."

The two men and Pauli made sounds of approval. Then, tucking in his shirt and brushing at his black pants, Pauli said, "I never got so close to a horse in my life, but that one—she's primo."

Flashing a shaka, he hurried back to the restaurant.

Thirty minutes later, Darby and Cade should have been back at the ranch, but they were still working with the Appaloosa.

"Good girl, Jewel," Darby crooned. She stood at the mare's head, holding the short piece of sawed-off lead rope clipped to the halter. Cade worked to untangle the rest of the rope from the horse's knotted tail.

"This makes me feel bad," Cade said as the mare closed her eyes and shuddered.

"My offer to do it is still open," Darby said. "My fingers are smaller than yours."

"Yeah, well, I've already got scars," Cade said. "If you take a hoof in the face, Jonah'll put me off the ranch."

"No, he'd ask you what I did wrong." Darby's attempt to make Cade smile fell flat.

Both of them watched Jewel's eyelids close and quiver.

"Good girl," Darby repeated. "The second we're done, you're going to a nice grassy paddock where you can roll around. Then you'll feel better."

Cade freed the last piece of rope from the long reddish tail hair. He studied the rope as if it were something more, then said, "I think he's going to get rid of her."

"Richard? He didn't say that," Darby protested.

"Next thing to it," Cade said as they led the horse. "She has to 'earn her keep or find a home elsewhere.' It won't take more than an afternoon's work to get her used to bein' washed, but this is a tourist operation. They don't want to put in the time.

"And look at her," he said as the mare waited for him to go through the gate first. "After all this, she's still got fine manners."

When they'd turned Jewel into the enclosure, she stood watching them, still cautious.

Finally they walked away, and Richard rejoined them.

"Thanks again," he said. "Next time you want to buy some used equipment, I'll give you a discount." He laughed, then his face turned serious. "I was just on the phone, severing the connection between the Royal Hapuna Hotel and that guy. Turns out he was a friend of Mr. Mudge. I hope he didn't wreck the horse."

"Don't give up on her; I could work with her a little," Cade offered.

"I'm not really in a position to hire," Richard began.

"Wouldn't want anything for it," Cade insisted. "I

just hate to see a good horse wasted."

Richard looked skeptical for a few seconds. Then he nodded slowly and Darby thought he'd figured out Cade wasn't one for trickery. He meant what he'd said.

"I'll look forward to seeing you," Richard said. "Maybe Pauli can help. I thought he was just one of our local surfers, but he might have a knack for it."

They waved good-bye and rushed toward the truck.

"Do you know him?" Darby asked. "Pauli, I mean."

"No." Cade opened the driver's-side door and climbed in.

"You sure worked together well."

"He saw what needed to be done and did it," Cade said. And then, just because he knew it would annoy her, he added, "And, he *is* a guy."

"Yeah, like that explains it," Darby said, but she was thinking that when Pauli stood up for Jewel, it had nearly canceled out the fact that he hung around with a jerk like Tyson.

"Even if I could buy her, I couldn't afford to feed her," Cade blurted as the truck rolled over the 'Iolani Ranch cattle guard. "Me and Mom have our hands full repairing the house and replanting the taro, never mind feeding Honi and Joker when I move back out there.

"Besides, why do I need an Appy mare? Joker's not a stallion."

At the end of what was an exceptionally long speech for Cade, Darby was excited. "You *could* do that! My gosh, Cade, you're so determined. Look how you're doing that long-distance learning thing—"

"Correspondence classes," Cade corrected.

"The repairing and replanting, I mean, you work that hard at 'Iolani all the time, and you've learned stuff from Jonah, haven't you?"

Cade flashed her a look that said she'd have to be dumb to even ask such a question.

"I mean about raising horses," Darby explained. "So, why not start an Appaloosa ranch?"

"That takes a few horses," Cade said, but his eyes turned almost dreamy, like he was seeing a view from the front porch of his ramshackle home where trampled taro was replaced by pastures polka-dotted with sleek Appaloosas.

"Start small with this mare," Darby urged.

Cade wrenched the steering wheel right, avoiding a series of corduroy-close road ruts.

"I just said I couldn't afford to feed one more," Cade snapped. "Catch a clue, Darby."

Darby didn't blame him for hiding his longing, but she couldn't let Cade get away with acting so superior.

Darby crossed her arms and said, "You'd better grow a mustache if you're going to start acting like my grandfather."

* * *

When they got back to the ranch, Cade and Darby unloaded the saddles and bridles onto a tarp stretched out in front of the tack room. The hooks had been put up in the tack room and labeled with each of the cremellos' names, but the gear had to be fitted to each horse before it was hung up.

The Western saddles were heavy and a little unwieldy for Darby. The sun-warmed leather was hot too, but as she staggered under the burden of one of them, she was distracted by the sight of Jonah, Kit, and Kimo having lunch with Medusa.

At least that's what it looked like, though maybe she was just hungry for lunch. The aroma of ginger, soy sauce, and noodles tantalized her almost as much as her curiosity. Why were the men all standing outside the corral at the end of the road, watching the steeldust mare?

Cade must have been wondering, too. Once they'd finished unloading, he poked her with his elbow and nodded for them to go check out the gathering together.

"We had some excitement," Darby announced as they walked up.

A quick flick of Medusa's ears showed she didn't welcome the two new humans, but she didn't flee or charge the fence. She only watched them through her black forelock.

Darby considered the progress Kit had made with the mare yesterday, when she'd finally allowed him to touch a brush to that mane. Today, Medusa's black mane still looked dull. It had rolled into dreadlocks that would be impossible to brush out. Would it have to be shaved like the manes of the horses at the Royal Hapuna Hotel?

"Excitement, huh? Mudge make you take a horse along with the used tack?" Jonah guessed.

"No, but it was close," Cade said.

"Mr. Mudge doesn't work there anymore," Darby explained, "but we met this great Appaloosa."

"Of course you did," Jonah said, but he seemed to have lost interest. He forked noodles into his mouth as he studied Medusa.

The mare backed into a corner and gazed toward the ranch office. Aunty Cathy had been known to take Inkspot and Blue Moon in there for a midday nap.

As if the wild mare had read Darby's thoughts and heard herself being accused about caring for the weanlings, Medusa snorted and pawed the red dirt.

"I hate havin' her in Hoku's corral still," Kit told Darby.

"It's okay."

"I'm moving her along as fast as I can without wreckin' her," Kit said.

"She knows," Jonah said.

So much for sympathy, Darby thought.

"Let's get back to what you were sayin' about those cremellos on the trail," Jonah reminded Kit.

"I'm no dude wrangler," Kit said.

Jonah snorted. "Who is?"

"Seems like if we don't want to damage the horses or land, we won't have people ride head-to-tail, day-after-day over the same track."

Darby realized they were all nodding.

"I'm thinking you, me, Kimo, Cade, and Cathy each plan trail rides. That gives us five different routes. We vary the horses and, uh, guides each day. That way the horses will have to pay attention to riders' commands, riders will have to listen to us, and we won't be cuttin' crisscrosses into the land," Kit said.

"We'd need to spread out," Jonah agreed. He held his arms apart and Medusa skittered away, then turned her rump to them all and lifted a hind hoof. "These crazy mares."

A sympathetic noise slipped from Darby, but she didn't argue because Kit was grinning.

"Did you see that? She was sneakin' up, listenin' to me talk 'til the boss opened his arms."

He was encouraged by Medusa's curiosity and Darby knew he was right. Even that cocked-hoof gesture was a good sign. Medusa used it with Inky and Luna Dancer when they demanded too much attention.

"There's still lunch for anyone who wants it," Megan yelled. She hung out the front door of Sun House.

"Go eat," Jonah said. He gathered the brightly lacquered bowls from Kimo and Kit and handed them along with his own to Darby. "Then get busy with those cremellos. Cathy wants us to trial-run 'em tomorrow morning. You, too, Cade. Megan made lunch, but it's good."

Cade ducked his head at Jonah's teasing. It was only a millimeter or so, but then he added, "I'll get something inside," and strode off to the bunkhouse before anyone could try to change his mind.

Megan refused to give Darby a fork or even a spoon to eat her noodles.

"We're learning to use chopsticks this summer," she insisted, placing two bowls and two sets of wooden chopsticks on the table.

"Why?"

"It's a useful skill," Megan said.

Darby slipped past her friend, headed for the silverware drawer. That was a major mistake, since it sent Megan into basketball mode with arms outflung. She feinted side to side, blocking Darby even when she'd stopped.

"Can't I learn a useful skill when I'm not weak from hunger?" Darby asked.

Megan lifted Darby's right arm by the wrist. "You're not shaking," she said, then angled a chopstick into Darby's hand. "Pretend you're holding a pencil. No, like this."

"Just give them to me," Darby said. "I'll figure it out."

About halfway through her bowl of noodles,

Darby quit pouting. Megan was totally oblivious to her grumpiness, anyway, and she couldn't wait to tell her about Jewel and the awful trainer.

"He doesn't sound like much of a trainer," Megan observed after Darby finished recounting the events. "More like a bronco buster in the old West. Isn't that what they called them? Going around from ranch to ranch, breaking a dozen horses in a day?"

Darby shrugged, not about to rush her hard-won mouthful of noodles. Even though her T-shirt wore traces of lunch, she'd been working harder at this ever since she'd remembered a reason to try.

Her mother was a whiz at eating with chopsticks. She'd demonstrated her expertise dozens of time by plucking a single grain of rice from a carton of takeout Chinese food.

Maybe, Darby thought, she'd surprise Ellen the next time she visited. And that was supposed to be soon, in a week or so.

By the time she'd finished and changed into a clean T-shirt, Megan had set up something else.

"Now, you get to choose your horses," Megan said.

"I thought your mom assigned them to us," Darby said.

"She doesn't care," Megan said as she held an empty, washed peanut-butter jar in one hand while she dug into her pocket. She came up with a bunch of little slips of paper.

"I wrote the cremellos' names on these," she said, tipping the papers off her palm and into the jar. Then she replaced its lid and shook it an excessive amount, considering there were only six names inside. "Now, we'll pick our horses, taking turns, of course, and when we're done, we'll go outside and match them up with their descriptions, and try on all their new-old tack."

"You turn everything into a game," Darby said. When Megan looked offended, she hurried to say, "And it's fun!"

"I'm just a jock at heart," Megan said. "You go first."

When they each had three slips of paper, they opened them and Darby learned her three summer charges were Cash, Maggie, and Makaha.

"And I've got Charisma, Pastel, and Windy," Megan read off the slips. "You know these are just their barn names," Megan said as they walked outside, "like Windy is really East Wind, and Cash is DashforCash, but the vet records Babe gave us say the horses all answer to their barn names."

"And they actually have kind of a barn," Darby said.

"According to my mom, they had to have shelter because some of them are photosensitive."

"Really?" Darby said. "I guess it makes sense. With their light skin, they might not be able to take a lot of sun."

She hadn't paid much attention to the cremellos' new home until today. It was sort of a keyhole-shaped enclosure. Three-quarters of it was grassy pasture but the narrow part that pointed toward the highway was roofed and had single stalls and a gate that could close off the grass, leaving the horses under cover to be fed.

Because Megan hadn't had time to halter all the cremellos, it took about two hours to fit the cremellos with halters, saddles, and bridles. Darby loved working with the horses and learned more about them in that afternoon than she had during the whole time they'd been on the ranch.

Darby considered "her" two geldings and mare. Maggie was about fourteen hands high, Cash was about fifteen, and Makaha was probably sixteen, although he looked a lot bigger, standing taller than any of the other pale horses.

Since she knew Cash best, Darby started by approaching him with a halter. When she flipped the lead rope over Cash's neck, Makaha snorted and trotted farther off. Maggie crowded close and lowered her head.

"No, I'm starting with him," Darby said. Holding the lead rope loop around the gelding's neck, she reached up and buckled the halter.

As she led Cash, she felt the liquid flow of his gait. Milk-white and mannerly, he was built like a running Quarter Horse and did everything she wanted him to do, before she even asked. He lifted each hoof as she reached for it, but when she lay the hoof pick aside, Maggie rushed in to pick it up with her lips. She swung her head back and forth, taunting Darby to come and get it.

"You could hurt yourself with that," Darby scolded, and the mare dropped it.

Cash stood solid even though Darby fumbled her first throw of the saddle she'd chosen for him. He didn't fidget when she snugged up the breast collar he'd need for carrying guests up and down the hills, and he didn't jump when Maggie nudged the gate closed with a slam, then looked to see if Darby was watching.

"You're next," Darby promised the mare.

When Darby carefully swung into Cash's saddle, he didn't seem surprised. She rode one circle of the pasture at a walk, then took him up to a trot. Maggie fell in alongside, then flattened her ears and whipped her tail at Cash. The gelding just lengthened his stride, and when Darby asked for a lope, he left Maggie behind.

"You read my mind like Navigator," Darby told him as she dismounted, and Megan, in the process of untacking one of her horses, gave Darby a thumbs-up.

Maggie was the prettiest of Darby's horses. Her flaxen mane and tail shone against her creamy hide and when she turned at just the right angle, the sun picked out dappling that looked like golden leopard skin.

The mare had a sense of humor, taking the bit then spitting it out before Darby could lift the headstall. She nuzzled Darby's neck and breathed deeply, learning her scent.

The halter and bridle Darby had put aside for Maggie fit fine, but she had a little trouble with the saddle cinch.

The girls had been working quietly, getting to know the horses as Jonah recommended, by watching, listening, and touching, but Megan looked over when she heard Maggie's grunt.

"If she's too chubby, we have cinch extenders in the tack room," Megan said.

Darby shushed her. "I just picked the wrong size. It's not like she's a pony." Darby gave the mare a pat and told her, "I'll find something suited to a full-grown horse."

Megan smothered a giggle and turned away. The next saddle Darby tried fit well enough. Standing on her toes, Darby gripped the saddle horn and cantle and moved the saddle while she watched the cinch, making sure it wouldn't chafe the beautiful mare.

It looked just right, and Darby was about to put her left boot in the stirrup when Maggie's head swung around and her lips grazed Darby's back pocket.

"Hey," she said before remembering.

Though Cash had been too polite to bring it up, Maggie was reminding Darby that she'd put some carrot chunks in her pockets. What were they there for, after all, if not for a sweet-tempered mare?

"When we're finished," Darby whispered.

Maggie allowed Darby to mount and put her through her paces before she looked longingly at the pocket again.

"You're funny," Darby told the mare once she'd untacked her, because even as the carrot juice drooled from Maggie's mouth, she watched Darby and nodded in gratitude.

Makaha had watched all the grooming and fitting of the other horses from a distance, and he wanted no part of it. Without breaking out of a walk, he stayed ahead of Darby so that she couldn't halter him.

When Megan finished with her last horse, she noticed Darby's predicament and came to help her.

"Now you're outnumbered," Megan told the gelding.

After that, he allowed himself to be cornered and haltered.

"I saved the last of the carrots for him, but he wasn't interested, " Darby told Megan.

"Not all horses are motivated by food," Megan said. "Tango sure isn't. She'd rather run than eat."

Megan's rose roan mare was Hoku's best friend in Hawaii besides Judge, the aged bay gelding who'd come all the way from Nevada with her.

"If I ever get to work with Hoku again," Darby said, "let's try riding her and Tango together and see how it goes. This morning when the burglar—"

"Lost tourist," Megan corrected.

"*Whoever* was around, Tango and Hoku stood together like they were ready to take him on."

"Good idea," Megan said. "If Kit wasn't so busy, I'd have him watch me with Tango. Something's going on in her head that wasn't there before she ran wild, and he's the only one I know who's worked with wild horses."

Megan leaned against the fence and watched as Darby brushed Makaha.

Darby had never been able to visualize the expression "raw-boned" but she thought Makaha might suit it.

Although he was sixteen hands high, she'd bet he didn't carry any more weight than little Maggie. He didn't look skinny, just very lean.

When it was time to fit his bridle Makaha held his head high.

"Is he afraid or just resisting?" Megan asked.

"I'm not sure," Darby said, but the way Makaha blinked each time the headstall neared his eyes made her worry that someone had abused him.

Like Hoku. Darby longed to finish up and go to her filly. The owner who'd tried to break her to saddle as a yearling had probably beaten her, even around the face. He was probably as bad as the "trainer" she'd seen today.

In the end, Makaha got his carrots as a reward after he accepted the mild snaffle bit and the gentle lengthening of the headstall.

Darby didn't mount Makaha right away. She and Megan petted and talked to the gelding.

"You'd say he was white until you saw this blaze," Darby said quietly to Megan.

"Or saw him standing next to Cash or Charisma," Megan agreed.

Makaha was tawny, with a faint brick color to his mane and tail and a bit of a Roman nose.

By the time Darby was astride the gelding, he'd forgotten about his reluctance. Moving smoothly into a running walk, he carried Darby around the pasture, alert for her signals.

"He's gliding," she told Megan as they passed by. Makaha's gaits were as easy and predictable as Navigator's. He'd be the perfect horse for adult men who came on the rides.

Megan had been waiting for her to finish. Once Darby had turned the gelding out to grass with the others, the girls carried the saddles, bridles, and halters down to the tack room and hung each item on the hooks and saddle trees labeled with the cremellos' names.

Megan stood with her arms raised and fingers locked, swaying to stretch out her hard-worked torso, and Darby was closing the latch on the tack-room door when she heard spurs ringing behind her.

She turned with raised eyebrows to face Kit.

"So, guess what, *keiki*?" he asked.

Darby smiled. Kit and Kimo had nicknamed her the can-do *keiki*, or can-do kid, and the name gave her a jolt of confidence each time she heard it.

"What?" she asked.

"Me 'n' Jonah come to an agreement," he drawled. "You've been so generous to Medusa, even puttin' Hoku out of her corral, that we can't stand by and let you lose all the ground you gained with your own horse."

Kit stopped talking. Was she supposed to know what he meant by that?

"Thanks?" Darby figured she couldn't go wrong being polite.

"Jonah's assigned me to work with you and your filly every day after I finish up." He made a sweeping gesture that took in the buildings, horses, vehicles, and everything else on the ranch.

Darby didn't know what to say. Kit was a real horseman. He knew and liked mustangs. Many evenings, though, she'd seen Kit's and Medusa's silhouettes against the dusky sky.

"Isn't that when you work with Medusa?" Darby asked.

"Thing is, the darker it gets, the better she likes me," Kit said.

Darby didn't think he was just saying that to be nice. She remembered her first weeks on the ranch with Hoku. They'd done their best work together at night, with only an owl for an audience.

Still, this was going to make awfully long days and short nights for the foreman. He was in charge of practically everything.

"Yep, we'll work Hoku from soon as you finish dinner until we lose the light. Not sayin' I'm not tired by the end of the day, 'cause I am, but you'll be doing most of the work with Hoku. I'll just be watchin'.

"And my girl? I'm comin' to think horses are nocturnal. Look at their big eyes, to collect the starlight, and don't they look reflective like cats' eyes? I'll have to ask Cricket about that. Or Dr. Luke."

It took Darby a few seconds to realize the "girl" Kit was talking about was Medusa. He might be an adult with tons of responsibility, but he cared for Medusa just as she did for Hoku.

"Soon's I have her standing calm to be haltered *a hundred percent of the time*," Kit said, shaking his index finger, "I'll put her in with the cremellos, so she'll have a herd to boss."

That could take forever, Darby thought, but then she reconsidered. Kit was an expert. It would probably take him half the time to train Medusa compared to the time she was spending with Hoku. But then, maybe a horse who'd never been trained would be easier to teach than one that had been broken by abuse.

Darby could hardly wait for Kit to help her with Hoku. She glanced toward the sun. It must be about five or six o'clock now.

She didn't know how long her mind had been wandering until Kit said, "If you don't think it's a good plan . . ."

"I think it's a great plan!" Darby's pulse beat so hard she felt it in her temples. "When do we start?"

"How about tonight?" Kit asked and Darby gave a cowgirl yell of delight.

Chapter Five

How cool is it that I'm temporarily excused from after-dinner chores? Darby thought as she gathered the folding chair, boom box, and book Kit had said would be part of their first training trick.

Juggling the odd assortment of things, Darby left Sun House and saw Kit was already waiting for her.

"We need something to pique her interest," Kit explained when she reached him at the head of the trail down to the broodmare pasture. "You'll just sit in the pasture on your chair with a boom box for noise and a book to read until it's dark."

Now she saw what Kit had meant about her doing most of the work. Only, it didn't sound much like work, either. Sit there and read while the music played?

"What will that do?" Darby asked.

"We'll see," Kit told her. "You'll either be part of the scenery to Hoku, or she'll wonder why you're acting different than she's ever seen you before, and come to investigate."

"Ohh," Darby said. If she knew Hoku, the filly would definitely come close enough to see what her human was doing.

"If she does come over, don't get up. You can talk to her and use her name, but don't move any more than you have to turning pages, and don't look at her."

They'd do this for several days, Kit explained, and then add in a stroll around the pasture, hoping Hoku would follow. Once she did, Darby could scratch Hoku's withers, groom her, and do whatever else she thought would rebuild their friendship.

"I'll just be here for supervision," Kit said, but then he gave a mysterious wink and added, "at first."

Darby liked the sound of that. She had a feeling Kit would teach her something cool. In fact, her friend Samantha, back in Nevada, had told her that Jake, Kit's brother, had taught her to give her horses secret names. Darby hoped it was something fun like that.

As the broodmare pasture came into view and she saw Hoku standing alongside Tango, cropping grass in the shadows, Darby said, "She looks happy."

"Hoku can't help likin' it, so don't sound so gloomy.

Horses on grass are livin' the way they were born to. If they're not prone to sunburn, bugs, or rain rash, it's best for 'em, too—exercisin' and eatin' when they want, and bein' part of a herd."

"So maybe I shouldn't move Hoku back to the corral?"

"You need to, for her own good," Kit said. "Keeping her a two-minute walk from Sun House means you can train her whenever you have a little time. You can make sure she doesn't get in any fights or accidents. You can keep her feet picked out and cleaned up and get her used to not minding. And that's just from your pointa view.

"Lookin' at it from her side, she likes hay, she likes you, and she gets to do interestin' things. A smart horse'll get bored just grazing all day."

This is going to work, Darby told herself. Her spirits lifted as they walked along and her ponytail swung from side to side.

"Did Cade tell you about that trainer in Hapuna?" Darby asked when they were almost down to the pasture.

"Yeah. Men like that ruin horses. Shan Stonerow"— Kit glanced at Darby, and her frown must have told him he didn't need to remind her who he was—"used that trick. I never saw it, but my grandfather did. Bewildered the horse *and* hurt it, he said." Kit's eyes squinted almost closed as he studied Hoku.

They walked in silence until Kit went on, "Never

missed a chance to give a horse a 'good stout stick right between the eyes.' He said they'd by-golly never forget him, after that." Kit spoke bitterly. "Hoku's lucky she got clear of him when she did."

Why did people like Shan Stonerow and the mean trainer even exist? Darby wondered.

When they reached the pasture gate, Kit kept Darby from opening it.

"Before you carry your gear in, forget about that ugly stuff." He rubbed rough fingers over her frown. The gesture reminded Darby of her father, but Kit was serious, not sympathetic. "Erase it from your mind, *keiki*. Just live in the now. That's what these mares do." He nodded at the horses. They drifted toward the gate because they recognized friends. "Got it?"

"Got it," Darby answered. She slipped inside the pasture, set up her chair, and settled down to read.

At the end of a half hour, Darby was surrounded by horses.

A dream come true, she thought. Even though they'd nudged her for food and found her pockets empty, the mares and foals stayed nearby. Their coats were gilded with the setting sun and they ignored Hoku's huffs.

Lady Wong gave a sigh so deep, it shook her dapple-gray body. Then she lay her head atop the book in Darby's lap, so that her ears could be scratched, and Hoku's patience snapped. She came right up behind Darby and breathed on the nape of her neck.

"Hey, Hoku, girl," Darby said as she kneaded the base of Lady Wong's ears. "I think we should go for a ride sometime soon, don't you?"

Hoku didn't answer, but Darby felt body heat radiating off the filly. She refused to leave while Lady Wong was being touched.

Lady Wong eventually backed away and shook her head. Hoku stamped, and then Darby heard the grinding of the sorrel filly's teeth as she set upon the grass.

Kit's chin rested on his arms, which were crossed on the top rail of the fence. The way his black hat shaded his eyes, Darby couldn't tell if he was awake or sleeping.

"You don't have to stay with me," Darby said. "Why don't you go up to Medusa?"

Kit's chin pivoted on his arms and he might have been looking up to the ridge where they'd seen the intruder.

"I feel better staying down here," he said.

He couldn't believe the intruder was going to come swooping down here again, Darby thought, but his wariness gave her the creeps.

Later, as they walked up the dark trail toward the welcoming lights of Sun House, Kit told her she'd made some progress with Hoku.

"Don't stay up too late tonight," Darby told Kit when he began explaining his midnight plans for Medusa.

"That's right, the Girl Scouts come tomorrow," he said.

"And Aunty Cathy wants us to do a dress rehearsal before they get here," Darby said.

Tacking up the horses and riding them out after they'd each filled out a sign-in form sounded like fun to Darby, but she seemed to be the only one who thought so.

"Lucky for me I'll be holding down the fort. While you all ride out, I'll be watching Medusa with the foals to see that she don't act up. And I'll be doing the same when the real guests get here," Kit said.

"Why? Just the noise?" Darby asked.

Kit caught his breath and looked at her from the corners of his eyes. He seemed to be sizing her up, deciding whether he should tell the truth.

"Some wild animals, when they feel threatened?" Kit began. "They kill their young so they won't get attacked by whatever's after them."

Darby thought for a moment. She'd heard about big cats—lions and tigers, for instance—doing that, but she'd thought it was a myth.

"How does that make sense?" Darby asked. She was watching Kit's face and waiting for an answer when she heard a pop, like the blowout of a tire.

She might not even have noticed if Kit hadn't startled at the sound. And then he did something sort of weird. Instead of looking toward the highway where the pop must have come from, Kit glanced back over his shoulder. Toward the ridge again.

He looked worried, and because of that, so was she.

During the forced rehearsal the next morning, every human was supposed to play let's-pretend. Darby didn't know what everyone else was doing, but while she and Megan readied the cremellos for the pretend guests, the dogs pretended to be crazy.

Jack and Jill paced the driveway. They looked beautiful, with their black coats brushed and shining, but every few minutes Jill would sit down and howl. Then Jack would paw at her and bump her until she stopped. Then they'd pace down the driveway again, until Jill began to howl.

As Megan and Darby led pairs of brushed and saddled horses out to the hitching rails, Sass harassed them. The blue merle nipped at Cash's heels and then at Charisma's. He dodged Makaha's well-aimed kick and when Maggie paused to sample a tasty weed, Sass rushed her. If she hadn't jerked her head up quickly, he might have bitten her nose.

Bart and Pip simply took turns barking. Bart stood in the ranch yard, barking, staring upward as if he could see through the upstairs apartment walls, while Pip yapped from inside.

Ashamed of them all, Peach rolled his eyes, yawned, then pulled himself under the bunkhouse for a nap.

Megan and Darby were the last to fill out the required guest forms for riding, so with all the horses saddled and ready, they hurried toward the office. On their way, they met Jonah.

"What are we going to do about the dogs when people are here?" Darby asked.

"Some people are afraid of dogs," Megan pointed out, "and Sass is acting like a jackal."

"I'll talk to them," Jonah said.

They were inside the office when Megan asked, "Do you think he meant the dogs?"

Darby shrugged and they rushed through the paperwork, finishing at the same time, then scurried back to the spot where Kit was helping each rider into the saddle.

Cade was mounted on Makaha, Kimo on Cash, and Jonah on Windy. Aunty Cathy had just settled into Pastel's saddle and she was grilling Kit.

"Now what?" she said, acting like a beginner who needed help in every single step.

"Hold your reins in your left hand, just below the knot," Kit said patiently.

"While my mother's being a head case," Megan whispered to Darby, "which do you want? Charisma or Maggie?"

They were the only two riderless mounts.

"Maggie," Darby told her.

Megan gave her a thumbs-up, and barely touched her toe to her stirrup as she swung onto Charisma. Megan landed so lightly, Charisma probably didn't even notice, Darby thought, admiring her friend's skill.

Darby had just noticed how well-behaved the dogs were being when Aunty Cathy realized both girls were on horseback.

"You were supposed to wait for Kit," she scolded.

"Sorry, Mom," Megan said. "We didn't want to waste time."

"I just—" Aunty Cathy brushed her blond-brown bangs away from her eyes as if they were obscuring her vision on purpose. "Everyone needs to understand what they're supposed to do."

"I'll stay behind to man the phones and make sure Medusa and the dogs don't go rogue and eat somebody," Kit said.

"You're not funny," Aunty Cathy said.

"No, ma'am," Kit agreed.

As the six riders left the ranch yard, Megan reined her horse close to Darby's and asked, "Do you think Kit's really staying behind to answer phones? Or is Jonah making him stay because he doesn't want the ranch untended with a prowler around?"

"Who knows?" Darby answered, hoping Megan would let the subject drop.

"If it really is someone trying to steal horses," Megan speculated, "he must be pretty dumb. Instead of slipping in here at night to 'case the joint,' he could have come along on one of our rides and we would have given him a guided tour."

"I wish you hadn't thought of that," Darby told her. "Now I'm going to be looking at everyone suspiciously."

"Yeah, you gotta keep an eye on those Girl Scouts," Cade said, and both girls gave surprised laughs. They hadn't noticed Cade sneaking up on them.

They rode out into a cloudless morning. Wet grass made the horses prance, and a sea wind smelled of salt and flowers.

As they rode, though, Aunty Cathy talked. It was clear she'd spent a sleepless, nervous night trying to anticipate everything that could go wrong.

"This is new terrain to the cremellos," Aunty Cathy said, "and they're sure to get some surprises. We can't count on them to be perfect."

"Never can," Jonah joined in.

"Guides will do all the opening and closing of gates, the dismounting to pick up litter—"

"This isn't Chicago," Jonah snapped, but then he softened and asked, "What litter?"

"Well," Aunty Cathy stalled. She scanned the pristine green hills. "Anything that could potentially make horses shy or cause an injury."

"Like what?"

"Anything! A shingle could get blown off the roof in a storm. Or a feed sack might not be disposed of properly—"

"Ouch," Darby complained. Months ago, Jonah had accused her of nearly poisoning Navigator by leaving old sacks with rotting grain in the bottom where he could get to them. "I don't do that anymore."

"I didn't necessarily mean you." Aunty Cathy

sounded apologetic.

"A dog could chase a horse," Cade suggested.

"Pig could spook 'em," Jonah added.

"I've got one!" Kimo said. "So, we're keepin' all the horses together, at a walk, but one hotshot hangs back 'cause he wants to gallop, yeah?" Kimo gestured as if the scene played in his imagination like a movie. "Then he comes drummin' his heels on his horse, ridin' right up through the middle." Kimo leaned over his horse's neck in pantomime. "Runnin' poor Pastel like a—uh, like a wombat!"

They all laughed, including Aunty Cathy, who said, "I didn't want my worries to be contagious."

"What about young kids?" Cade asked as the laughter trailed off. "Do we allow 'em? Do they ride their own horse?"

"I've been thinking we'd pony anyone under ten," Aunty Cathy said, "and not take kids under eight."

Cade made a sound of agreement, but then Aunty Cathy began thinking out loud. "But what if that doesn't work because the child gets all fussy?"

"Tell him to settle down," Kimo answered.

"Jonah"—Aunty Cathy swiveled in her saddle—"will these horses carry double if we have a kid who's really scared and wants to ride with a parent?"

"I'm not letting Daddy Dude who doesn't know how to ride by himself ride with a kid," Jonah said. "Bad for the horse and the kid."

Aunty Cathy didn't seem to hear him. She pointed

and said, "Darby's the smallest. Let me see if Pastel will carry double."

Was she supposed to climb off Maggie and get up in back of Pastel's saddle? Darby looked helplessly at her grandfather, but it was Megan who came to her rescue.

"Mom!" Megan sounded concerned, not embarrassed. "You're making yourself crazy."

Aunty Cathy pressed her lips together and rode in silence for a few minutes.

"*Am* I acting crazy?" she asked Jonah.

"A pinch of *pupule*—who cares? But you can't plan for every trouble, Cathy, so you know that old song that says 'what will be, will be'?"

"I don't know it," Megan said.

"Is it Hawaiian?" Darby asked.

"Italian, I think," Jonah answered, and when Aunty Cathy let out an audible sigh, he assured her, "If this don't all come out right, it won't be because of you."

 Chapter Six

They'd been back at the ranch for about thirty minutes and though Aunty Cathy had cautioned everyone to save time to make themselves presentable, Darby and Megan stood in the office, staring at their chore lists.

Keep three cremellos groomed, healthy, and beautiful. *Check,* Darby thought.

Saddle "your" three horses each day they have riders. *Check.* She'd cooled out Maggie, Makaha, and Cash, and loosened their cinches so they'd be comfortable while they waited, tied by their neck ropes, for the Girl Scout troop to arrive.

Be the backup guide for trail rides. Darby didn't yet know if she'd be needed today. Judging by Aunty

Cathy's extra caution, they might all be riding along as guides.

Feed Pigolo, Francie, dogs. Check. She'd done that first thing this morning.

That only left *clean up after Pigolo, Francie, dogs* and *halter break Inkspot and Luna Dancer.*

That last one had to be a summer-long goal, not a chore. In any case, it wasn't going to happen in the next two hours, so Darby got a shovel and a wheelbarrow and set about doing cleanup.

"For a little goat and a pint-sized pig, you guys sure have busy digestive systems," Darby muttered to Pigolo and Francie.

And the cremellos were no better. Even though they weren't on her list, the white horses had not been very fastidious during their trips across the ranch yard. And horse droppings didn't make a good first impression.

The blue van that swerved then stopped in front of Sun House gave the impression of having been hijacked. Doors rolled open and girls spilled out, heading for the horses, before the driver had even turned off the ignition.

"I get that one!"

"That pretty one's calling my name!"

"Mine!"

Darby and Megan stood near the horses, cautioning the girls not to rush between them.

"Good call," Megan told Darby. "They're not just here for a merit badge. They really do like horses."

That was me this time last year, Darby thought. *Horse-hungry in every cell. And living here hasn't changed that.*

But it was the Girl Scouts' turn to fall in love with 'Iolani Ranch's horses and Darby's time to get down to business.

She wasn't going along on this first ride—Megan, Aunty Cathy, and Kimo were today's guides—but she focused on the size and temperament of each girl and their leader. She was performing common sense matchups just as she had with the saddles and bridles, when she realized something.

"There are seven of them, not six."

"And one's not a girl," Megan said. She did her own head count, then confirmed, "Seven. Well, we don't have a shortage of horses."

"Aloha!" Aunty Cathy stepped out of the office with open arms, and a chorus of alohas echoed back to her.

Wearing a white shirt, khaki pants, and a flower tucked behind her ear, Aunty Cathy looked young and excited as she motioned the girls and their leader into the office.

"Mom looks great," Megan said. "She loves this hostess stuff."

"She makes me miss my mom," Darby said.

"She'll be here for the Fourth of July," Megan reminded her as Kimo, mounted, drew rein beside them.

"Me 'n' Kona are going down to get Judge," he said, nodding at the extra rider.

As he left, Darby got her first good look at the guy. He'd been talking to the Girl Scout leader, but now he hung back, just outside the office.

"Hey!" Darby blurted. "The one who's not a girl. I know him."

"I thought he looked kind of familiar," Megan said as her mother gestured that she needed help inside the office.

"Granddaughter! That Maggie's wandering away," Jonah snapped.

Darby went after the mare, and even though she stayed with the horses, checking cinches and breast collars, word filtered out to her from the office via Megan.

It turned out that Mrs. Akua, the troop's leader, was Pauli's mom.

"You guys got him all 'stoked' about horses yesterday," Megan said as she helped one of the girls onto Pastel and shortened her stirrups. "He thinks Jewel—that's her name, right?—is the most awesome thing on earth and that Cade being a full-time paniolo is, too."

Darby thought about that while she readjusted Cash's cinch. For some reason it was wrinkling his skin. She lifted each of his front legs in turn, and the wrinkling disappeared.

As Aunty Cathy was helping the young girls mount, Darby had to strain to hear Megan.

"Careful, honey, don't pull on that bit. It hurts—"

"I guess Pauli talked to his uncle who said all this stuff—"

"—no, don't cry. Pastel's okay—"

"—about paniolos being men of skill and dignity, and not letting nightfall stop them from chasing wild cattle—"

"Just give me your hand. See?" Aunty Cathy said. "You can pet his mane and he'll forget you pulled his mouth."

"So, he's riding along as a chaperone," Megan finished. She patted the little girl's leg, looked up at her, and said, "Your horse's name is Windy."

A chaperone? Hadn't Pauli said yesterday that he'd never been so close to a horse? That had to include riding one.

Darby turned toward the sound of hoofbeats. Here came Kimo, leading Judge, but she wasn't thinking about them.

This morning Megan had tossed out the idea that anyone who wanted to look over the ranch for underhanded purposes could just book a horseback ride.

Now, here was Pauli, showing up unexpectedly.

Pauli was Tyson's friend. Tyson's record of fighting and vandalism were no secret. It wasn't much of a stretch to think he'd give horse thieving a try. And he'd need an accomplice. Maybe Pauli was just like Tyson, but he'd been lucky enough never to have been caught.

Darby was ashamed of herself. It wasn't like her to make assumptions about anyone, but she couldn't shake that stupid proverb out of her mind, the one that said, *Birds of a feather flock together.*

Pauli and his mother were arguing, and even though they kept their voices down, Darby heard enough to realize the disagreement was over wearing helmets.

"No way. None of *them* have helmets."

"Girl Scout rules dictate wearing them for safety reasons."

"Mom? I'm not a Girl Scout."

It was then Darby realized she wasn't the only one eavesdropping.

"He's our mascot!" squeaked one of the girls. Her wistful smile said she probably had a crush on him.

Pauli nodded toward Megan, Aunty Cathy, and Kimo, but she could tell he was really looking at Cade. The young paniolo had just ridden up the steep trail on Joker. Flushed from the ride, he vaulted from the saddle. To Pauli, he must have looked free, unbound by rules.

"Mom, I'm not trying to start anything," Pauli whispered, and Darby could tell he was embarrassed. Yesterday he'd been at work, in charge, a rescuer. Today, he had to ask permission like a little kid.

How does this work into his scheme? Darby wondered, but her attention was snatched away when the girl who'd mounted first grew tired of waiting. She clucked to Cash and flapped her legs until he moved away from the others.

Megan strode after her, but the child had kicked Cash into a trot. Megan picked up her pace. As she jogged, her baseball cap blew off. The little girls clapped.

But then the runaway Girl Scout disappeared from her mount's back. Cash halted and waited for Megan to catch up.

"Help!" came a voice and Darby realized Cash's saddle had slid to the left.

"That's what happens if you don't wait for us to tighten your horse's cinch," Darby answered the children's gasps.

That sounded like a threat. Darby winced, then added, "Your guides will tell you when to ride. Your guides are Megan," she pointed, "Kimo, and Mrs. Kato."

"Cathy," Cathy corrected, "and we're almost ready to go."

Bart had been very well-behaved until now, and that was probably why Darby noticed his whine.

"Things will settle down soon, boy," Darby told the dog, but he ignored her and kept staring toward Two Sisters.

Darby was just thinking that anyone could get away with anything during all this commotion, when Kimo handed her Judge's reins. The gelding was brushed, saddled, and he even smelled good. Kimo had sprayed conditioner on his forelock so he could brush out the tangles.

"Thanks," Darby said.

Now that the gelding was ready, what about Pauli? Was his mom going to let him ride without a helmet?

She didn't ask.

"Judge is a Nevada cow pony. He lived on Deerpath Ranch," Darby told Pauli as he approached.

"So, what's he doin' here?" Pauli looked different than he had yesterday. His blue T-shirt had a wave on the front and what she'd taken for hair dye on his cockatoo crest was really sun-bleaching. Just like her black hair, his turned reddish from too much sun.

"Judge came over on a ship, with my horse."

"Which one's yours?" Pauli looked around.

"She's down in a pasture," Darby said. "You'll see her on your ride."

Darby could have kicked herself for revealing that, but Pauli didn't act like a thief. She was trying to puzzle out whether he was or wasn't when he stroked Judge's flank.

The gelding only swung his head around to see who'd touched him, but Pauli jumped back, startled.

"You just surprised him," Darby said, "and their flanks are ticklish." Pauli extended his hand for the horse to smell. "See?" she said as Judge did exactly that, then his brown eyes studied the boy.

Pauli could hardly talk through his grin. "Yeah, we're cool, aren't we, Judge? I'm just, well, more used to surfing than riding. Honest, I didn't even really know this place was here."

A stray memory told Darby that people who said *honest* before a sentence were lying. Had she read that in a book that was fiction or nonfiction? It could make a difference. And how could he not know a ranch of two thousand acres existed?

"We're off," Mrs. Akua said from Makaha's back, and though there'd been nothing more said about helmets, Pauli stayed behind while Aunty Cathy, Megan, Kimo, and all the Girl Scouts rode away, accompanied by two Australian shepherds.

"Need help with anything?" Pauli asked sheepishly when it was clear work had stopped all around him.

Darby couldn't tell what Jonah and Cade were thinking, but *she* thought being so stubborn you missed a ride was silly.

Still, she offered, "I'm going to go work with two foals. You can watch if you like." She heard the half-heartedness of her offer. "I'm sorry you couldn't ride."

"Me too," he said, hand flat on Judge's bay cheek.

Darby's suspicions left her feeling guilty. Judge trusted him.

"If you wanna ride, ride." Jonah strode toward them, as gruff and bossy as he'd been on the day of Darby's first ride.

Pauli gave Jonah a slow nod, glanced at Cade, who appeared to be watching Joker at the watering trough, then turned to her. Pauli's expression was two parts excitement and one part alarm.

I know just how you feel, Darby thought. She led Judge to the side hill and explained how to mount.

Pauli settled into the saddle as if he belonged there.

Jonah tugged at Judge's saddle blanket, straightening it. Then he stood in front of the horse to make sure all the gear was square. Darby noticed Pauli's frayed-hem jeans hung over leather sandals with tire-tread soles. She knew just what Jonah was going to say.

"Don't come back here wearing any shoes without heels," Jonah told him. "I don't want you getting dragged to death on my place."

"No, sir," Pauli said.

Jonah smoothed one side of his black mustache as he looked Pauli in the eyes. Just like Judge, her grandfather appeared satisfied with what he saw.

Two out of two, Darby thought. Were her suspicions wrong?

"Cade." Jonah looked at his *hanai*'d son and shook his head. Joker stood behind Cade and his muzzle was still wet from drinking, dripping a small downpour on Cade's hala hat. "Take Pauli holo holo."

As Cade remounted Joker, Kit sauntered within earshot of Pauli and Darby and said, "Tell ya a secret. When I work with that wild mare at night? I wear a helmet."

"You do?" Darby asked.

"A wild mare at night," Pauli echoed in admiration.

"Are you a paniolo, too?"

"He's a bronc rider," Cade explained. "He's done some big rodeos."

"Ex-bronc rider," Kit stressed. "One bronc crippled my arm and I do okay, but I don't see how I'd get along if another one cracked my head."

"For sure," Pauli agreed.

"Go through the fold, then keep 'im on the flat," Jonah ordered. He nodded toward the end of the road. "And away from the little girls."

Was that code for "keep him out of his mother's sight"?

Darby knew Aunty Cathy wouldn't approve of this defiant ride, but the guys looked so pleased as they rode off on Judge and Joker, she didn't blame Jonah for letting them go. Cade didn't have any friends off the ranch, and if he'd made one, Aunty Cathy would have to approve of that.

Peach bumped against Darby's legs, then looked up with a canine smile. The dogs had been great, despite the noisy children.

"Good dog," Darby said as Peach followed her to the round pen, where Kit had placed Inkspot and Blue Moon. She'd thought it would be a good idea for her to work with them while they were in with Medusa, but Kit and Jonah had forbidden her to get that close to the wild mare.

Laughter came from the fold. It was just a little dip, then rise in the grass, Darby thought, but on her first day of riding, it would have terrified her.

"I bet Pauli's mom will be ecstatic about his new friend," she told the dog. "Even if Cade has a rough background, he's an angel compared to Tyson."

Darby had been with the foals for nearly an hour, just letting them get used to her nearness, when Peach bounded away with a single bark, greeting Cade and Pauli.

Bolting the gate behind her, Darby watched Pauli slide off Judge. His legs shook from the unaccustomed position, but he kept his feet beneath him and a grip on his horse's reins.

"What should I—?" he began, but Cade dismounted and took Judge's reins from him.

"*Mahalo*," Pauli said, rubbing his hands on the front of his jeans. "Now, show me what to do next."

"I'll do it," Darby said.

"He wants to learn *all* about horses," Cade told her. Then he stripped the saddle from Judge, set it in Pauli's arms, and pointed out the rack where it belonged, inside the tack room.

"Man's work," Pauli growled. He lifted the Western saddle like a barbell and swaggered in to put it away.

While Pauli was inside, Cade turned to Darby and said, "You will not believe our plan."

Darby's mind darted from tricking Pauli's mother, to getting Pauli boots, to—oh, please no!—bringing

Tyson to the ranch to make a Hawaiian Three Musketeers.

"I might believe it, but I sure can't guess it," Darby said as Pauli emerged from the tack room.

"You two talking stink about me?" he asked, then curled his right arm and admired his tanned, but not-so-big bicep.

"Our plan," Cade said.

"It's primo," Pauli said, "and I'm pretty sure we can pull it off." He bowed to Darby as if she were part of an invisible audience, saying, "Thank you. No, really, hold your applause, please."

Peach's tail swung against Darby's leg in appreciation.

"What is it?" Darby asked, but then Peach's head turned and his ears perked up at the sound of approaching riders.

"Later," Pauli said. His face took on a hangdog look and he asked, "Do I look miserable enough?"

"For what?"

"For a guy who's been sitting around with nothing to do while the Girl Scouts got to go riding," Pauli said.

"I guess so," Darby said, but Pauli was already talking to Cade and Jonah, who had just come up, saying there was something about riding that reminded him of surfing.

"Balance," Jonah said.

"Maybe," Pauli said thoughtfully. "One thing's for sure: It's good fun."

Flush-faced and swaying with their horses' steps, the riders came into sight.

"Let's see if this makes things simpler for the *keiki*," Jonah said, picking up a stepladder. He carried it over to the mounting and dismounting area.

Behind the tired but smiling Girl Scouts, Aunty Cathy gave them a thumbs-up.

 Chapter Seven

That night, dinner was frozen pizza and carrot sticks. No one complained, not even Megan, who lifted her slice with chopsticks and tried to take a bite as it wobbled.

Though the day's work hadn't been strenuous, the newness of it had been, and even Jonah looked drowsy.

Darby welcomed the cool breeze. She'd read that people could get sunburned through their clothes, but she hadn't actually believed it until today.

Not that she'd looked. She was afraid if she took off her clothes for a shower, she'd be too floppy afterward to go down and work with Hoku. And now that she'd begun her boom-box-and-book desensitization program, skipping a night was out of the question.

"How did Hoku act when you all rode past the pasture?" Darby asked. "Did she think you were a herd she should join?"

"She acted like a queen. Hardly looked at us, but didn't run away, either." Megan crunched a piece of crust.

"Elbows," Aunty Cathy said, pointing at her daughter.

Megan set her chopsticks aside. She folded her hands in her lap and then collapsed, cheek down, on the dinner table, pretending only her elbows had held her up.

Darby laughed, even though Jonah said, "Don't encourage her."

When Darby met Kit to walk down to the broodmare pasture, the expression on his face was totally out of character.

"What's up?" she asked.

"Nothing much." Kit tilted his head down a little so that his hat brim obscured his face.

Darby didn't push it. Kit looked like he was holding in a secret. It probably had nothing to do with her. Even though Kit was her friend, he was also the foreman. He'd tell her if she needed to know, but she couldn't help being curious. He had a look her mother would compare to a cat who'd swallowed a canary.

Darby set up her chair and boom box in the same

place in the twilit pasture. She was reading a fantasy story about a shape-shifter. Without looking at Hoku, she wished she could change into a horse, canter over to Hoku, and tell her that she hadn't meant to neglect her.

That didn't happen, but Hoku welcomed Darby's company. Examining the same grass she'd checked out the night before, the filly came closer and closer.

Within an hour, Hoku grazed within touching distance. Darby kept reading and humming along with the radio until she glanced over at the pasture fence. Kit's small gesture indicated she should stand up.

Should she move slowly, in tiny increments, or just stand up?

Hoku's teeth paused in their grinding. Even though she didn't lift her head, the filly's eyes shifted toward Darby.

"I'm not going to give you time to think too much," Darby sang. She stood, placed her hands on the small of her back so that Hoku knew she wouldn't grab for her, then stretched.

Hoku didn't move her feet, but she extended her nose toward Darby and sniffed. Darby took mental stock of what she had in her pockets. No sugar cubes or carrots.

"This is all you get, *ipo*," she said. The endearment Aunt Babe had used for Hoku, a shortening of the word for *sweetheart*, just seemed right. "Eee-po." Darby drew the word out and Hoku sneezed in her direction.

The sneeze seemed like encouragement. So, moving

slowly as if she were underwater, she walked close enough to give Hoku's shoulder a pat and then, following Kit's unspoken directions, she left.

Since she couldn't stand the suspense of wondering what Hoku was doing, Darby approached the gate from an angle and strained her eyes to their corners.

It looked like Hoku was staring after her.

Progress, Darby thought. And then she heard Hoku's trotting hoofbeats.

She was following! Drawing closer, catching up, then passing by.

Darby stopped and Hoku came to her. She didn't look nervous or coiled to escape. Her walk was relaxed and loose. Her head bobbed and muscles slid beneath her sorrel satin skin. She nickered, tossed her head toward the gate, and Darby got the feeling her horse was saying, "Let's go," not, "Get out of here."

Darby decided to end on a high note. Instead of trying to clamor up onto her filly's back and ride, which is what she really wanted, she just slipped out of the pasture. "See you tomorrow."

"Perfect," Kit said when she reached him. "Couldn't be better. You'll be riding her tomorrow."

Darby's heart sang as she skipped up the path to the ranch yard.

"Pretty happy?" Kit asked.

"The only thing wrong is that it ended too soon," Darby said.

"Thought you were tired."

"I was, but now I'm—" She paused for the proper word, almost said *stoked*, and settled for, "Revitalized."

"Good," Kit said. "How 'bout if I introduce you to Medusa? She's got a teacher. Now, she could use a friend."

Though she wasn't sure how Kit expected her to make friends with the wild steeldust mare, Darby agreed.

Selfishly, she knew that the faster Medusa became tame, the sooner Hoku would be back in her home corral, closer to her. But that wasn't why Darby said yes. Kit was helping her to win Hoku's heart back. She'd do anything he asked.

Kit set aside his Stetson. "By friend, I just mean another human she's used to seeing close-up. I don't want you going in with her, just watch for a minute," he said, clicking the snap of a helmet closed under his chin. "And let her smell you."

"I aim to please," Darby joked, but just before Kit entered the corral with Medusa, Darby saw the mare's head lift, her nostrils flutter, and Medusa was looking straight at her.

The sun was just going down, and even though Medusa was used to Kit's approach in the darkness, she began rearing.

Darby thought there was a rehearsed quality to the mare's performance. Sure, her deadly hooves were within inches of his head, but the dark fury in her eyes was missing.

Darby gave herself a mental shake. Even if the mare was doing what she always did, she wasn't playing. This was a dangerous routine.

When Medusa came down to earth, Kit stopped walking toward her.

It was a little reward for the behavior he wanted, Darby thought, but it also made Medusa watch to see what he'd do next.

Kit put his hands in his pockets.

Medusa swung her head away, but her body didn't follow. An instant later, she took a single step toward him. It looked like an accident, as if her weight had just shifted in his direction, but when the mare's ears pricked toward Kit, Darby knew it wasn't.

This time Medusa's reward was birdsong.

Kit whistled. No, it was better than that. He imitated a meadowlark, reminding Darby of the warbling birds that lived in the one field near her house in Pacific Pinnacles.

Each time the mare looked his way, Kit answered with the meadowlark's call and words Darby heard but couldn't understand.

The mare blew through her lips. Medusa found the birdsong familiar and soothing. So did Darby. She didn't realize the busy day, her success with Hoku, and Kit's quiet training had led her to doze off until the foreman woke her, and sent her home to Sun House and bed.

* * *

Darby was a little groggy when she wandered into the ranch kitchen the next morning. But then Aunty Cathy told her she'd be leading her first tourist ride and she was totally awake.

"Wow! Leading?" Darby said. "When? How many of them?"

"Your Aunt Babe called last night while you were out with Hoku. She said there'd just be four, a married couple and their children, so I thought it would be a good opportunity for you to try leading," Aunty Cathy said. "How about a one-and-a-half-hour loop toward the Two Sisters pasture, with Megan riding in back, keeping watch on the children?"

"That's so cool!" Darby looked toward the ceiling, wondering if Megan was up yet.

"I'll get her," Aunty Cathy said. "Your group will be here at ten, so that gives you enough time to tend to your chores and pick some horses. If you need me, I'll be in the office, catching up.

"Oh, and if you see Kimo before I do, tell him Jonah and Kit are out rounding up some steers that took it into their bony heads to push over a section of fence. Then they'll be mending the fence."

"Not their favorite job," Darby said, but she was too excited to be pulled down in sympathy.

"And after that, they're repairing the last of the earthquake damage so that they can get set up for the crew that's coming in to start on your new house."

Aunty Cathy said it casually, as if they'd been

talking about it all week.

"Already?" Darby asked.

"Sure," Aunty Cathy said, "unless you think your mom wants to spend the rainy season sharing your room." She kissed Darby's cheek, then said, "Now, don't keep me here all day talking story."

The day couldn't get any better, Darby thought.

As she fed the animals, Darby imagined herself aboard Navigator, kindly but firmly advising the guests to avoid any paths because they wanted the horses paying attention to them. As she wielded her shovel between the ground and wheelbarrow, she pictured herself pointing out Hoku as they passed by the broodmare pasture.

"Yes, that's my horse," she'd say as Hoku ran along the fence line with streaming gold mane and tail.

"Hey, Sleepin' Beauty!"

Darby's head snapped toward the bunkhouse, where Kimo and Cade stood talking.

"You wanna bring your shovel over here?" Kimo called. "I've got some—"

"None of our guests will be going over there," Darby shouted, "so you can do it yourself! Oh, and did Cade tell you—"

Kimo nodded. "Fence repair," he said, shuddering. "Who says gettin' to work on Hawaiian time is a bad habit?"

Kimo looked festive in a bright yellow shirt and

Darby wondered if she'd missed the announcement of some holiday. Father's Day was coming soon, but Kimo wouldn't dress up for that.

"Why do you look so nice?" she shouted to him.

"Good jeans!" he yelled back, and that confused her until she figured out that he'd meant *genes*.

By the time Darby had haltered Maggie, Windy, Cash, and Pastel, Megan was not only up, she was outside, zipping around on an ATV.

She slowed near Darby and the four horses.

"Two lead ropes in each hand," Megan said and nodded admiringly.

For the hundredth time, Darby thought, *if I could have seen into the future this time last year and glimpsed myself leading four white horses, I would have believed I'd gone to heaven!*

"What are you doing?" Darby asked.

"I'm going to get Tango. Want me to catch Navigator, too?"

"If he's not already on his way up," Darby said. "He seems to know when we're going for a ride."

Megan revved the ATV a little too loudly for Windy. The gelding startled into the other horses and Pastel gave him a bite.

"Hey!" Darby shouted as Windy raised a rear hoof to retaliate.

"Sorry!" Megan said. "I'll tell Hoku you said hi!"

Darby had the cremellos brushed and tacked up and she was working on Navigator when Aunty

Cathy hurried out of the office.

"You've got one more coming, sorry!"

Navigator tossed his head, black with rusty rings around his eyes, as if he were protesting.

"Hey, Gator, you don't have to carry anyone but me." Darby looked around for Jonah. He didn't believe in pampering horses, but she couldn't resist giving Navigator a quick kiss on his muzzle.

The heavy Quarter Horse had been Darby's "babysitter" from the day she'd arrived on the island, and she hadn't picked him; he'd picked her. It seemed to be his goal to make her beginner's riding skills look better than they were.

"Size and shape?" Megan asked her mother. She was already astride Tango, putting the rose roan mare through her paces in preparation for the ride.

"An adult man. He says he's ridden 'plenty,'" Aunty Cathy offered.

"I'll get Makaha, yeah?" Megan asked, and Darby nodded.

Concentrating as she picked out Navigator's feet, Darby thought she'd mount the parents on Windy and Pastel. Those two horses were in something of a mood. With luck, she could count on adults to keep them apart if they started bickering.

She'd put the oldest child on Cash and the nine-year-old on Maggie, because the little mare was patient and good-tempered.

* * *

It turned out that Robin, a pigtailed girl with a gap where her front teeth had been, was just as friendly as Maggie. At first she clung shyly to her father's leg, but when they came out of the office after signing the forms to ride, she held out a ruined lei.

"She wants her horse to wear it," the father said helplessly.

Anyone with a grown-up's perception of size could tell the circle of flowers wouldn't fit over a horse's head.

"Hmm," Darby said. For a minute she concentrated on the lei. Its white blossoms were crisscrossed with brown creases.

"She's been sleeping in it," the mother explained.

"Your horse is Maggie," Darby said, "and she's a little too big to wear that, but you know who it would fit? Francie."

As soon as she said it, Darby knew it was a mistake, so she added, "But Francie's a goat and she might eat it!"

"What do you think, Robin?" the father asked.

The whole time Darby had been pointing out Maggie and Francie, the little girl had kept her eyes on Darby's face. Now, she extended the lei toward Darby. "You wear it!"

"Me?"

Robin whispered to her father and he whispered back, then told Darby, "You get to wear it because you're a real cowgirl."

Robin pressed her hands over her mouth and gazed up at Darby, starstruck.

"Yes, she is," Megan said, and she leaned down from Tango, took the lei from the little girl, and dropped it over Darby's head.

It smelled wonderful, and the child's compliment was even sweeter.

Darby and Megan stalled while waiting for the fifth rider by teaching the guests all their horses' names, and memorizing the guests' names. *Bob and Carol, Robin and Gary,* Darby repeated the names to herself over and over again. Usually, she was pretty good with names, but today she was nervous.

Even after the entire family was mounted up, the extra rider still hadn't arrived.

"We have an afternoon sea kayak tour," Carol, the mother, said. "I don't know how punctual they'll expect us to be."

"So, we'd better get going." Darby agreed with the mother's unspoken concern.

"Can the dog come?" Gary asked.

"Sure, Sass is very good around horses," Darby said, but she raised her eyebrows at Megan, asking if they should leave without the fifth rider.

"Go ahead," Megan told her. "As soon as he gets here, we'll catch up with you."

 Chapter Eight

At first, everything went even better than Darby had expected.

Ten-year-old Gary had taken riding lessons through a recreation program back home in Denver, Colorado.

"You're handling Cash like a real pro," Darby told him.

He turned to his little sister and said, "See?"

Robin didn't listen. She was too busy gazing at the far-off trees of the rain forest.

"Do you go in there?" she asked Darby. "Is it scary?"

"I go in there all the time and it's not a bit scary," Darby said. "My grandmother's house is in there."

"Like Little Red Riding Hood?"

"Robin, gee!" her brother moaned, then looked down. "She's dumb, huh, Sass?"

Pink tongue lolling from his mouth, the Australian shepherd looked up, fanned his tail, and kept trotting beside Cash.

"What if you got lost?" Robin insisted.

"It couldn't happen," Darby said. "My horse Navigator knows how to get home from any place on this whole island!"

Both parents gave her grateful grins, and Darby reveled in the green-and-gold day surrounding her. A yellowheaded bird, maybe a palila, darted overhead, and Pastel and Windy, who'd forgotten their quarrel, stared after it. Hoku and Kanaka Luna stood close enough to their fences that she could show them off, too.

She wasn't even worried about Megan and the other guest catching up. The man had registered late and was coming alone, so maybe he'd changed his mind.

Then she glanced back over her shoulder and saw them.

Even from this distance—about two football fields away—Darby could tell the man was at home on a horse. He and Megan were passing by the broodmare pasture, and Hoku, who'd been right at the fence, was gone.

Darby had expected Hoku to hang her head over

the fence to greet Tango, her pasture buddy. Instead, Hoku was galloping toward Pearl pasture.

The man pointed after her.

Nothing disturbing about that, she told herself, so why were misgivings moving like sticky-footed bugs down her spine?

Under the man, Makaha wasn't moving like his usual self, either. He jerked each hoof up as if they'd touched down on hot earth. His head was tucked in and tilted in an unnatural position.

Sass looked back, too. He didn't wag his tail as Megan waved and sent Tango loping toward them.

"Turn your horses around," Darby told her guests. She demonstrated, reining Navigator into an about-face. "This way, they don't just hear hooves pounding up from behind. We'll wait for Megan and our other guest to catch up."

"Sass, come back," Gary called, but the Australian shepherd stalked away.

Head lowered, hair rising across his shoulders, Sass stood in the narrowing gap between Darby, the family, and the oncoming riders.

"What's he see?" Carol asked. "Not a wild pig, I hope. We were warned about those."

"Just an unfamiliar person," Darby assured her.

"He didn't growl at *us,*" Carol observed.

"No," Darby agreed.

Sass's snarl changed from a warning to a threat.

Arrr, he growled, then drew in a wet-sounding breath.

Nose wrinkled. Gums showing. Teeth bared. Saliva dripped from the dog's mouth. For the first time ever, Darby was afraid of Sass.

"Call him off," Megan joked as they rode up, but then she got a good look at him.

Head held low, Sass advanced by inches. He stared with wolfish intensity, and he might have launched himself at the stranger if the man hadn't flicked the ends of his reins to startle the dog.

"Here to me," Megan ordered and Darby was almost certain the command would work.

She sure hoped so, since Tango was already rolling her eyes and the family had gathered their horses close to one another.

Sass went to Megan, but he directed a volley of barks at the man as he circled past. Reaching Tango, he sat, but he didn't settle.

"Someone should teach that dog some manners."

Darby looked from Sass to Makaha. She meant to look at the man, but her gaze snagged on the horse. Neck arched, mouth open, he held the bit as if it were made of thorns.

Darby had a quick impression of a thick, unhappy man on the white gelding, but it was his arrogant attitude that Darby recognized. The "cowboy" who'd tied Jewel into a pretzel, then frightened her with a hose, sat there on Makaha.

What was he doing here?

"Everyone, this is Mr. Stonerow." Megan introduced him, and Darby's confusion turned into a nightmare.

No. Darby's lips formed the word, but she didn't sound it. Buzzing filled her ears, even if no swarm of killer bees was crowding against her eardrums. Only her dizziness was real. She gripped her saddle horn for balance.

Then she squared her shoulders and purposely rested her right hand on her thigh, while her left hand held the reins.

She'd either misheard Megan or there were two men named Stonerow. No other explanation made sense, because a Shan Stonerow had once owned Hoku.

A Shan Stonerow had lived in Nevada. Ann Potter's father had known him there.

Is her face scarred? Mr. Potter had asked Darby when she'd revealed her wild filly's previous owner. *If Hoku was his, you're lucky she's not ruined . . . he beat the devil out of them.*

Why didn't Megan remember? She'd been in the car that day, too.

The rest of the ride passed in a blur.

Megan rode up beside Darby and hissed, "What is wrong with you? And Sass?"

Darby couldn't explain while they were riding so close together.

With a wide gesture, Megan sent Sass home, then engaged Bob and Carol in a lively conversation. She told Gary she was sorry she'd had to send Sass home, but if he couldn't control his bad mood, he had to be in time-out. Then Megan teased Robin, asking if she had sugar on her finger, because she put it in her mouth each time she looked at Mr. Stonerow.

Darby tried to think.

She wanted to ask Megan if she'd seen the man's first name.

Shan Stonerow rode his horses as yearlings. Way too young. *Shan* Stonerow had bought Hoku from Samanath Forster's friend's parents because their ranch had been going broke. And that cruel cowboy at the Hapuna resort had even said he was from Nevada. It had to be the same man.

They stopped to let the horses drink. Only Navigator refused to lower his head. Knowing his tension was probably her fault, Darby tried to sit loose in her saddle, but it was too late for that.

Navigator gathered beneath her as if he might bolt. Bands of muscle tightened and his ears flattened. Darby leaned forward and gave him a pat on the neck, but the gelding wasn't comforted.

And Bob, the dad, the man she was supposed to be treating as an honored guest, wasn't fooled. As they left the water, he called Darby and motioned for her to ride next to him.

"Hey," he said quietly, "do you need me to make

a citizen's arrest or something? I think I can take him."

Bad, Darby thought. On the first ride she'd ever led, one guest was offering to jump another.

"No, of course not." Darby forced out a laugh, then whispered, "If I'm a little crabby, it's because he's late! Hey, look up there! I think that's a *pueo.*"

"What?" Carol said.

"I don't see a pay-o." Robin twisted in her saddle.

Darby didn't, either, but she got a nod of approval from Megan as the older girl rattled off facts and stories about the Hawaiian owl. It was the Kealoha family's *'aumakua,* she said, bound to protect past, present, and future inhabitants of the ranch.

"That includes the horses," Darby said, and she really hoped she was right.

No one was working within sight of the house as they rode back in. The ranch yard was so quiet, Darby heard Pigolo make a happy grunting noise as he rooted around in his pen, but no human sounds came from Sun House, the office, or the tack room.

Where was everyone? Darby had been watching for Jonah or Kit or Aunty Cathy, keeping her back turned on Shan Stonerow and hoping he wouldn't notice her distress.

"Are you dehydrated?" Megan whispered as she and Darby helped Gary and Robin dismount.

"No, I'm fine," Darby said in an undertone she

hoped the kids wouldn't hear.

Megan obviously didn't believe her, because she pinched up a piece of skin on Darby's upper arm.

"Ow!" Darby yelped. She knew if the pinch of skin stayed up, it indicated that she needed water. Megan was looking out for her, but Darby couldn't imagine a worse time to get such a painful and annoying tweak. "I said *no*!"

"I insist." Carol smiled and extended tip money to Darby and Megan.

"Thank you, so much," Megan said.

"Thanks!" Darby echoed. "I hope you'll come back again. In fact—" Darby had almost forgotten the lei around her neck. She lifted it off, slipped it on Robin, kissed the little girl's cheeks, and told her, "If you throw the lei into the ocean when you get back to the beach, and it goes out to sea, it means you'll come back to Hawaii."

"Mommy, did you hear?" Robin bounced with eagerness. "Let's go!"

The family waved as they walked to their car. Jonah's truck was gone. So was Kimo's.

Darby had to tell Megan, in case she needed her help.

Darby dropped to her knees by Navigator's front hoof.

"Sis, take a look at this!" She didn't have to fake her urgency, and Megan was beside her, instantly. "Keep looking down and just listen."

"You need some wa—"

"Just listen." Darby rose into a crouch and lifted the big gelding's hoof onto her knee. She swept her index finger around the hoof wall as if something was wrong there.

"That guy used to own Hoku."

"What's he—?" Megan exhaled at Darby's pleading look, then gasped as she remembered. "Shan Stonerow?" she whispered.

"The same guy who hurt that Appy in Hapuna," Darby said, nodding.

Megan's eyes widened, then her gaze darted over Darby's shoulder.

"I see what you mean, but he'll be fine." Megan raised her voice, still pretending to talk about Navigator's hoof. "They Super-Glue cracked hooves like that all the time."

Shan Stonerow had dismounted, so Megan rushed over to him.

"I'll take Makaha." Megan sounded overly cheerful as she took the reins from him. "Did you have a good ride?"

"Good enough," he said. He worked his hands into the back pockets of his jeans, but his stance didn't match the watchful way his eyes scanned the ranch yard.

All at once, Darby thought of Jonah's library under the stairs. It would be a great hiding place, if she could get inside the house.

Are you that scared?

No. She'd never slip off and leave 'Iolani's horses without her protection, no matter how puny it might be.

"You have a nice day, now," Megan said as she led Makaha away.

Shan chuckled as if she'd said something funny, then nodded at Darby. "I need to talk to your associate."

"Okay," Megan said, shrugging. "In a couple minutes; I need her help."

The girls loosened cinches, slipped off headstalls, and hung them on saddle horns.

"When we're finished, I'm going to go see what's up with Pip," Megan said. She glanced irritably toward her upstairs apartment. Darby didn't hear anything, so maybe Megan was thinking Aunty Cathy had left the ranch office and gone upstairs. She might be using Pip as an excuse.

At last, all the horses were tied by their neck ropes.

All except for Navigator. The big gelding squealed and sidestepped when she started to unbuckle his cinch.

"I've never heard him do that," Megan said.

"Me either."

Navigator switched his tail and moved off. Certain he'd stay nearby, Darby let him go. If nothing else brought Jonah out of hiding, that would. She'd definitely just let Navigator have his own way.

But what if Navigator knew something she didn't?

Darby left him saddled and bridled, just in case.

Chapter Nine

"Be right back," Megan said. She jogged toward the house as gracefully as any human in cowgirl boots ever had, but Shan Stonerow didn't notice.

"I want my horse back."

If he'd socked her in the stomach, she would have felt the same as she did at that moment. And, just as if she'd had the wind knocked out of her, Darby couldn't speak.

But maybe it wasn't as bad as it seemed.

What if he was here on vacation? He'd heard 'Iolani Ranch was open to guest riders. Then he'd seen Hoku, recognized her by the marking on her chest, and put that together with gossip he'd heard in Nevada about the filly leaving the alkali and sagebrush for Hawaii.

After seeing how beautiful the filly had become, how could Stonerow not want her back?

That scenario included way too many coincidences, but Darby decided to believe it.

"Sorry," she told him firmly. "I'll never sell her. Ever."

He gave her what might have been a pitying look from another man. She'd noticed his sneer before, but now she could see where it came from. The corners of his mouth were squared off, but on the left side of his face a wrinkle made a deep parentheses from his nose to the corner of his mouth.

He must have expressed his scorn thousands of times to get that engraved on his face, she thought.

"I don't want to buy her," Shan Stonerow told her. "I've tracked her all the way from Nevada. She's my horse. I'm giving you a chance to return her to me, before I go to the police and have you arrested."

Shan Stonerow turned at the sound of Megan coming back down the stairs. Clearly Aunty Cathy hadn't been in the apartment or she would have been right behind her daughter. But Megan had thought of something else. As soon as she reached the ground, she seemed to pour Pip out of her arms.

The little white dog could always be counted on to cause an uproar and today was no different. Pip's yapping brought three Australian shepherds sliding around the corner of the bunkhouse.

Give her to me . . . police . . . arrested . . . The dogs

couldn't help her against Stonerow's threats, but she was glad to see them.

Kit and Cade looked as bad-tempered as Sass as they appeared behind the dogs. The cowboys' smudged clothes and hands reminded Darby that they were working on earthquake damage to the bunkhouse.

They hated indoor work, especially in such warm weather. Even Cade had complained—out of Jonah's hearing—that some repair stuff called Spackle would get all over them and the bunkhouse.

She'd bet that's what the smeared white stuff was.

Megan must have switched to sneakers when she went upstairs, because she was sprinting after Pip and caught him. As she swept the small dog off his feet and into her arms, the Aussies jumped after him.

From where Darby stood, it seemed Megan looked pointedly between Kit and Cade, then Darby and Shan Stonerow. Darby wasn't sure that the cowboys understood, but the dogs did.

In a whirlwind of black and white, the Aussies streaked toward Stonerow. Sass circled him with lowered head and raised hackles, while Jill barked and Bart played "gotcha" with Stonerow's boots.

Bart was the youngest of the Aussies, about eighteen months old, and still acted like a pup. He only had two expressions—impish and ashamed—and right now he was definitely impish. He rushed in to nip at Stonerow's feet, then swerved away to circle him at a tail-tucked run.

He looked silly, but not as silly as Stonerow, who pretended he wasn't at the center of a pack attack.

"I know you're softhearted about horses. I'm not. I don't mistreat them, but I do keep them in their place as animals. Still, if it makes you feel any better, I won't be keeping the filly. I have a buyer who saw her on the TV news and he likes her nerve."

Kit had already pulled on his black Stetson. He brushed Spackle from his clothes as he strode toward them. Cade was trying to keep up, and, uncharacteristically, he was talking a mile a minute.

He must have recognized Stonerow as the man who'd terrorized Jewel. Was he warning Kit to look out for Stonerow's cruel ways?

After a day's worth of work he hated, Kit looked intent on mayhem. Until he recognized Shan Stonerow, too, and pulled up short.

And then, maybe Bart got in a too-hard nip, or maybe Stonerow had just had enough of being a chew toy, because Bart yelped, thrown sideways by a kick.

All of the other dogs worshipped Jonah, but Bart had bonded with Cade. The dog scuttled straight to Cade. Looking ashamed, he licked Cade's hand in apology.

Cade might have hurled himself on Stonerow, if Kit's outstretched arm and three words—"I'll handle this"—hadn't stopped him. Anyone could see the young paniolo was hoping for blood.

If Stonerow recognized the hatred aimed at him, he ignored it.

"Jake Ely! Good to see you." He rushed forward with his right hand outthrust. "Here to do some horse tradin'. Your boss allow that?"

No, Darby thought, *Jake is Sam Forster's friend.* Kit was the oldest of the Ely brothers and Jake was the youngest. And that crack about his boss was designed to make Kit get all puffed up and say *darned right* he was allowed to do some horse tradin'.

But none of that happened.

Kit kept coming. He didn't bother to correct Stonerow. His angry expression faded into something blank and cold. When he stopped about five feet away, he crossed his arms.

Darby was pretty sure both men were Shoshone, but their tribal resemblance stopped at their dark skin and black hair. Kit looked like a proud archer. Stonerow looked like a guy who made secret deals with the cavalry.

The two stared at each other.

In the silence, Darby could hear the horses. Maggie leaned down to rub her neck on the hitching rail, groaning when her itch was scratched. The minute stretched into at least three. Windy and Pastel revived their quarrel by shoving against each other, and the bits on their headstalls jingled.

Darby's toes curled inside her boots and her fingers tightened into fists. Stonerow was going to lose this stare-off, but when?

"It's not the human way to just give up something

you care about," Shan said. He sighed as if he'd been holding his breath all that time. "I've been lookin' for my horse a good year."

"What horse'd that be?" Kit asked.

There was the sound of truck tires hitting ruts, spinning up gravel, going too fast on the ranch road. It must be Jonah or Kimo.

Stonerow didn't seem to notice the noise. His voice, as he answered Kit, sounded like a storyteller's.

"Her name is Smokin' Kitty," Stonerow said, "because she's so fast."

Darby's breath caught. That wasn't her name, but he was right. Her wild filly ran on winged hooves. Why did this cruel man know that? How had he forced her to run?

"Her name also speaks of her color, bright as a brushfire burning, and of Princess Kitty, her dam, and her sire, Smoke, a gray mustang." Stonerow's sneer deepened before he said, "Old stud bred better foals than anyone had a right to expect."

Tires going too fast hit the cattle guard at the end of the ranch road.

Kit rubbed the back of his neck, but didn't say anything.

Jonah's brown Land Rover bucked into sight and braked to a stop in front of Sun House. Dust swirled around it, but Darby could still see the pale owl painted above turquoise lettering.

Jonah got out of the truck and strode toward them.

His black mustache curved up above his smile. He clasped Stonerow's hand in a grip that surprised him into taking a step backward.

Then he pounded his shoulder as if they were the best of long-separated friends and said, "I hear you're a stranger in paradise. Welcome to 'Iolani Ranch."

Stonerow's jaw actually dropped in amazement.

Chapter Ten

Shan Stonerow recovered quickly, shaking Jonah's hand with something like respect, but it took Darby a little longer.

What could her grandfather be thinking? She tried to see the situation as he did, getting out of the truck.

He'd seen Shan Stonerow in jeans, boots, and a Western snap shirt, apparently having a conversation with Kit. Just a regular guy, maybe a horseman.

But Kit's arms were still crossed, Cade had a bright flush along his cheekbones, and Megan was hovering over Bart, clearing her throat as if she were trying not to cry.

And me, Darby thought fast. Maybe he'd misinterpreted everyone else. What could she do to show

Jonah that Shan Stonerow was a bad guy?

Darby's thoughts ricocheted inside her brain. At last, she stood on tiptoes, so he'd be sure to see her, and did the only thing she could think of: She drew her index finger across her throat.

Her grandfather definitely saw.

Taken aback by such a violent gesture, Jonah stared at her with a confused frown.

Megan was still clearing her throat. Darby glanced toward her and saw Megan nodding toward her apartment. Then, she held her hand up in a shaka.

But, no. That's not what she meant. Megan had her fingers tucked against her palm, but she raised her hand until her thumb touched her ear and her pinky was by her mouth.

"Jonah, you got a filly, name of Smokin' Kitty?" Kit asked.

But Darby still watched Megan. What did she mean? Apparently it wasn't supposed to be very complex, because Megan was rolling her eyes in disgust.

All at once, Darby got it. Of course. When Megan had gone upstairs to get Pip, she'd called Jonah on his cell phone.

"Smokin' Kitty? No," Jonah answered his foreman.

For a fraction of a second, Darby considered Stonerow and thought five against one wasn't fair.

But then she thought of Jewel, trying her best to please this man when he only wanted her to fear him. And Hoku, head-shy and so fearful of men she'd actually struck Cade in the chest so hard it scarred him.

"We're both businessmen," Stonerow said to Jonah, "and we know the true value of a horse is what someone's willing to pay for it. Example: Some folks don't bother about bloodlines. They want a loud-colored horse. They'd pay more for a paint cayuse twenty years old than a plain brown Thoroughbred that just won thousands of dollars."

Jonah nodded as if he appreciated Stonerow's wisdom.

"Lately, I've met up with folks who collect horses like they do fine art. They want a notorious horse, involved in a deadly track accident, for instance. Or a celebrity's horse. An American League baseball player—you'd know his name—bought three prime warmbloods for his wife. When they divorced, he sold them to me for fifty bucks each."

Jonah didn't try to hide his disbelief. Stonerow noticed and continued. "Got to have documentation if people are going to believe you. Like the whatcha call it? On a piece of art?"

"Provenance," Darby suggested, then twisted her ponytail so hard it hurt. She hadn't meant to speak to him. The word had just popped out. And it was the right one.

Shan Stonerow did an air clap as if she were brilliant.

Just once, Darby wished she didn't have such a great vocabulary.

"You know Abyss, the rock star?" Stonerow asked. "The pony he rode as a kid paid my bills for six months. People couldn't wait to give me money for that old beggar."

"People are crazy," Jonah said.

"How do you *find* these horses?" Kit's question was barely audible.

Stonerow could have ignored it, but he didn't.

"It's a talent. Although it doesn't always work. It took me a year to find my horse."

Kit looked down at the dirt and shook his head. *So we're back to that foolishness,* his posture said.

"I saw her on television during tsunami coverage," Stonerow went on. "That's when my buyer saw her, too."

That was the second time he'd spoken of a buyer and all at once Darby saw the fatal flaw in Stonerow's scheme.

"I have adoption papers from the Bureau of Land Management," Darby blurted.

No one except Stonerow looked at her. He was smiling.

Let him think he'd tricked her into admitting Hoku was his horse. It didn't matter what he thought, because she *did* have adoption papers.

"I can even tell you who signed them. Brynna Forster." Darby nodded, proud she'd been able to fish Sam's stepmother's name from her memory.

"Brynna Forster doesn't work for the BLM," Stone-row said.

"She did then," Darby insisted.

"Even so, title to an adopted mustang isn't permanent until an inspection is done one year after the horse is adopted."

Is that true? Darby didn't remember.

Movement caught her eye. Past the round pen, past the place where Hoku had once been tangled in barbed wire, probably two miles away, Darby saw Aunty Cathy riding one of the cremellos. Both of them looked pretty in the hazy sunlight, but Darby wished Aunty Cathy was someone else. Brynna Forster, Mrs. Allen, or even Sam! Samantha Forster was only a few years older than Darby, but she knew everything about wild horses.

"Wonder how they transported the horse out of state without a bill of sale," Stonerow mused. "That's right, BLM marks 'em with a freeze brand. That shows they were wild."

Darby didn't know her hands were shaking until Megan left Bart and came up to comfort her. She only stood beside Darby, hands on hips, but it helped.

Maybe it was a coincidence that Stonerow looked beyond Megan at her horse.

Tango shone pink and silver in the late-afternoon light. Even though she was dozing, weight canted to one side with her eyes closed, she was beautiful.

"Tell you what I can do to kind of even things up

and take the sting out of you folks losing my filly. I'll buy that rosewater-colored mare, too." Stonerow pointed at Tango.

"Yeah! Try to take both of our horses!" Megan advanced on Stonerow as if he'd fouled her on the soccer field. "See where that gets you!"

Megan was literally in his face, at least her index finger was, when Jonah said, "Mekana."

His soothing tone worked like gasoline on a fire. She turned on him, answering in rapid-fire Hawaiian that made Cade suck in a loud breath.

"Go to your room," Jonah ordered.

Megan's mouth opened in a retort, but she hesitated, and Darby had never had more respect for her almost-sister.

Darby could see there was only one thing Megan wanted more than to tell Jonah he wasn't her father and had no right to treat her like he was. That one other thing was not to weaken him in front of Stonerow.

Darby could tell the instant her friend decided Jonah would have a better chance against Stonerow without her interference.

"Fine!" Megan said, and when she stormed toward the stairs to her apartment, Pipsqueak trotted behind her like a forgotten lamb.

As if he'd never mentioned Tango and Megan hadn't spoken up, Stonerow asked, "Was my filly showin' a freeze brand?"

Darby looked at Kit. He was from Nevada. He

knew about wild horses. Maybe he could explain what Shan Stonerow meant.

"A freeze brand is one BLM stamps on a wild horse's neck when it's brought in off the range," Kit told her. "It doesn't hurt 'em. It's just so super-cold it turns the hair white. From then on, that horse is marked as a mustang, and it wears a symbol showing its age, when and where it was caught, stuff like that. Usually."

"Always," Stonerow corrected.

Darby didn't want to hear any more. She'd shrugged her shoulders up so high, they almost touched her ears. She hadn't done that for a long time. And now she realized it didn't help. Just because she didn't hear Stonerow talking didn't mean he wasn't right.

"Wasn't it a special case, Granddaughter? The horse'd been hit by a bus?"

"Yes!"

"Not the best time for branding. At least in Hawaii," Jonah said. Looking over his shoulder to see Aunty Cathy riding up on Charisma, he added, "Could be things are different on the mainland."

Stonerow brushed aside Jonah's sarcasm. "It still invalidates the contract."

"What contract?" Aunty Cathy said. "I'm the business manager for this ranch." She looked at Jonah. "Perhaps this is something that I should be present for?"

Jonah's face flushed, but Darby couldn't tell if it was from embarrassment, anger, or pride.

"It's already kind of a free-for-all, Cathy," Kit said. "Jump on in."

The foreman's joke broke the tension, but his humor irritated Stonerow.

"Let me bring you up to speed," Stonerow said, but even when he'd done that and made it sound as if Darby was part of a theft, it didn't matter to Aunty Cathy.

"Darby is a minor. She couldn't enter into a contract alone."

"Want me to go get the BLM papers?" Darby asked, but Stonerow spoke over her.

"Did you sign it? Are you her mother, then?" Stonerow's gaze compared Cathy and Darby. Then he answered his own question. "No."

"Her grandfather is her legal guardian. Her mother's out of the country, but I could contact her if this situation warranted it."

There was another length of silence. When it became clear that they wouldn't just hand Hoku over, Stonerow asked, "Can I just take a closer look at my horse and check on how she's doing? I have photos of her when she was young. One's a close-up of the white star on her chest."

Darby didn't ask to see the photos. He'd take it the wrong way. When nobody else spoke up, either,

Stonerow continued. "I really love that sorrel horse, and I didn't know what happened to her for the longest time."

Darby wanted to tell him to stop, to quit using that wistful tone. She knew he'd beaten Hoku. You didn't hurt a horse you loved.

"How'd she go missing?" Kit asked.

As if this was the only question he hadn't rehearsed for, Stonerow's dark eyes widened and the curve between his nose and the left side of his mouth twitched.

"You know Monument Lake?"

Kit gave a quick nod.

"It's tribal land, cheaper to let her eat the tribe's wild grass than feed her in a pen. We all do it," he said. He winked at Kit, but the foreman didn't respond.

"The least you can do is let me see her," Stonerow insisted.

"Boss?"

Jonah yawned.

"Maybe tomorrow," he said. "I want a nap before dinner."

Before he faced another insult, Stonerow nodded.

"I think that's a good suggestion. I'll come back tomorrow, and we'll sit down, maybe at your kitchen table, and compare my documents with yours," he said, giving Darby an indulgent smile.

Shan Stonerow had started walking toward his car when Kit called, "Be sure to come on in the front way like you did today. The back gates'll be padlocked."

Stonerow turned and looked at Kit. He passed his car keys from hand to hand, a calculating look on his face, but he must have heard something in Kit's tone that signaled another, bigger confrontation, so he just nodded.

 Chapter Eleven

"I should have known," Aunty Cathy said. Darby and Kit were slumped into chairs in the ranch office, but Aunty Cathy was pacing while she talked about Stonerow. "I should have spotted him as a troublemaker.

"He was late. He balked at filling out the form because he was 'in a hurry.' Then, he made such a mess of his name that I asked him to redo it on the next line and print. I didn't check it, and look."

Aunty Cathy held out the list of guest riders. It was a measure of the deliberate mess Stonerow had made that the signature above his—nine-year-old Robin's— was more legible.

"Did he just expect us to *give* him Hoku?" Aunty Cathy didn't expect an answer. She stopped pacing and stared at the office clock. "It's too late to call BLM in Washington, D.C. It's two o'clock here. That makes it eight at night there."

Mind jumbled, Darby couldn't believe someone in Washington, D.C., would care about the fate of one little mustang. Even if Hoku's existence was recorded in a computer in some gray metal office, what good would it do?

"Just five in Nevada," Kit said. "Let's try Willow Springs Wild Horse Center."

Darby had never been there, but Sam Forster had told her about it when Darby had been in Darton County during those cold days before Christmas last year.

It was a place of corrals. Wild horses fresh off the range were trucked there and funneled into pens by age and sex, and, if they were lucky, by family groups. But Hoku had never been there. She'd gone directly from the frozen road where she'd been hit by a school bus to a cozy stall at Mrs. Allen's Blind Faith Mustang Sanctuary.

Focus, Darby told herself. *Hoku needs the best of your brain right now.*

"You think someone will still be in?" Darby asked.

"Last time I was there, the place was run by a fussy bureaucrat," Kit said. "Can't remember his name, but that don't matter. He could have the government's computer files open in a heartbeat."

He leaned over Aunty Cathy's shoulder as she went online to find the wild horse center's website. Darby didn't watch. What if those computer files had no record of Hoku? If she'd slipped through the bureau's system because her adoption was handled in an unusual manner, did that mean she still belonged to Stonerow?

"Norman White!" Kit read from the screen. "That's him."

"We could wait until tomorrow," Darby suggested.

"And let that *crook* get the jump on us?" Kit asked with a humorless laugh. "No way."

Darby covered her face with her hands. She wasn't crying. She just felt better to be in the dark.

"Honey?" Aunty Cathy asked.

"What if he's right?" Darby asked. "Hoku doesn't have a freeze brand. Brynna wasn't exactly working at the BLM. She was on leave or something. Maybe she even got fired. How do we know? And before that Hoku *was* his and if he has a bill of sale, even if it's old, does that prove Sam Forster's friend's dad—"

"You're afraid Hoku is legally Stonerow's." Kit managed to bundle up all her notions in a few words.

Darby nodded, but the admission hurt so much, it felt like her sternum might crack.

"I know he's our intruder from the other night," Kit said. "If he had proof she belonged to him, why risk breakin' in?"

"I'm calling," Aunty Cathy said. "Knowing is better than not knowing."

She dialed, waited, and when she spoke, it was clear it was to an answering machine. She left the ranch number and the numbers for her cell phone and Jonah's.

"Now, we wait," Aunty Cathy said, "and if Norman White is as fussy as you think he is, he'll hate a wheeler-dealer like Stonerow interfering with his system."

Darby was grateful. She should show it. Should hug someone or at least say something, but she felt like she had an energy leak. She could hardly move.

"I've never been the patient sort," Kit said. "Let me check with Jonah, see if I can get him to let us start early—right now, in fact—with Hoku."

"Okay," Darby said, but she couldn't imagine touching Hoku's satin skin for the last time.

"Jonah's at our place, talking to Megan," Cathy told Kit. "What could she have said to that toad Stonerow that got her in trouble?" Aunty Cathy looked genuinely confused. No one had had the time to explain yet, so Darby tried.

"It wasn't what she said to him. She said something to Jonah."

"What kind of something? He drives her crazy, but she loves Jonah."

"I don't think it was mean or anything. I think she was mad and maybe it was really rude, but I don't know. It was in Hawaiian."

"I told Ben that teaching his daughter a language I couldn't understand was a mistake." Cathy tsked her tongue, but she smiled at whatever she was remembering. "Those two were slipping secrets past me from the time Megan could talk."

"Jonah understood her just fine," Kit pointed out.

"Cade, too," Darby said, recalling his gasp.

As if he'd been waiting for Darby's halfhearted smile, Kit said, "The day's already trashed. Go on up to the house and get your stuff."

"No more riders today?" Darby asked.

"No, and none tomorrow," Aunty Cathy said.

"Okay," Darby said.

She started to leave, but Kit tapped her shoulder.

"This time don't bring your book and lawn chair," he said. "Put on sneakers, grab a helmet, and I'll bring the carrots. Meet me in Luna's pasture."

Luna's pasture? Darby didn't want any part of trying to train Hoku in the stallion's compound, but she said, "Okay."

Automatically, she left the office and went to Sun House, but when she sat down on the bench by the front door and tried to take off her boots, she couldn't.

Her fingers were stone-cold and so numb they didn't work. Finally, she used Jonah's bootjack, but even with the help of the tool it took several tries.

She padded down the hall to her bedroom. It felt later than two o'clock in the afternoon.

Sneakers, Kit had said. That was almost as weird as

meeting in Luna's pasture. But he was telling Jonah all about it. Or telling him something, because Darby could hear Kit upstairs, talking to Jonah from the doorway of Megan and Aunty Cathy's apartment. It was strange to hear the rough resonance of male voices up there.

It came over her like a crushing wave: Darby wanted her mother. She knew she should wait and tell her what was happening later, after she really knew what was going on, but she wanted her mother now.

Hang in there, Darby told herself, but it didn't help.

She stood in front of her bedroom mirror and said it aloud: "Hang in there."

She hated the way she looked in the mirror. Her eyes were too big for her face, like some kind of reptile. A gecko, maybe. Her mouth looked too soft, like it belonged on a little girl, not a teenager. Her hand went up and closed around the flying-heart charm on the chain around her neck, and Darby didn't see the gift from Jonah. She only saw her scrawny wrist.

She pressed her shoulders back, but her spine felt bowed from hundreds of nights fighting to get a breath.

She had permission to call Mom whenever she needed to, so she marched into the kitchen and dialed. She didn't know what time it was in Tahiti or how this emergency would fit into her mother's filming schedule. She just did it.

And her mother seemed to feel the same.

"He what? He did *not*!" Ellen Kealoha Carter's outrage matched Darby's. "Darby, you just tell that man that he's made a long, expensive trip for nothing. I signed those documents and I don't sign anything without reading it thoroughly. What a joke." Her mother's words oozed contempt.

"But I don't want to lose Hoku—"

"You're not going to. I won't allow it. Jonah certainly won't allow it and in view of what I signed, the federal government better not allow it!"

Darby felt better.

"Kealohas are never short of backbone," Ellen said. "Call me when you hear more."

"I will," Darby said, and when she left Sun House she was actually thinking Shan Stonerow didn't stand a chance of stealing her horse. If she had to, she'd just take Hoku and go into hiding. There were places in the rain forest and Crimson Vale where a *malahini* like him would never find them.

"I'm gonna show you how to ride like an Indian," Kit said. When they met at the top of the path he carried a leather bag, Hoku's halter with the tangerine-and-white-striped lead rope, and a sack of carrots. "It's what you horse charmer folk call a bonding exercise."

"Uh-huh," Darby answered. She knew Kit was teasing, but he'd never asked her to wear a helmet around Hoku before. That was a little unsettling. And where were the dogs? The Aussies were always underfoot unless they were locked up.

Down below, she saw Jonah in Kanaka Luna's vast pasture.

"Is my grandfather taking Luna somewhere?"

"For a backbreaker, he said. I think that's just a strenuous ride."

As they walked, Darby flashed back on the way Kit had confronted Shan Stonerow.

"Kit? Even before he started talking, you didn't like Shan Stonerow. Is it because of what we told you about that Appaloosa in Hapuna?"

"That," Kit said, "and he's opened his mouth plenty before today."

"What do you mean?" Darby pressed him. The prospect of some unfinished business from Nevada made her curious. "Is it something we can use against him?"

"Bloodthirsty this afternoon, aren't ya?" Kit said. "But I'd recommend you shake that off, or I won't be able to teach you to be invisible."

The gate to the stallion compound stood open when they reached it, and Kit wasted no time explaining what he had in mind.

"Plains Indians got a reputation for being able to appear and disappear by doin' this, but it's real simple."

Using the armload of leather scraps he'd brought along, Kit explained how to tie a strip of leather around a horse's barrel and ride with another leather strip knotted around the horse's lower jaw with a single rein.

"They used deer hide and called it a war bridle," Kit said, "and when they wanted to vanish—hunting or fighting—they'd slip to one side of the horse with a heel hooked on the leather and shoot arrows from under the horse's neck."

Kit paused, letting her picture the trick. Once it sank in, Darby said, "Pretty cool, but you don't think—"

"The horse became a shield," Kit went on, "and the rider was all but invisible. You could only see his bare foot or, now and then, the top of his head, and only if you knew what you were looking for."

"You don't really think Hoku would let me do that, do you?"

Kit's grin was like sudden sunshine.

"Oh, no, don't smile," she told him. "I'm not saying *I'm* going to let me do that!"

"The People used to do it barefooted and without a helmet; that's just plain terrifying."

"Yeah!" Darby agreed.

"And I don't want to lose my job over this."

"That's comforting," Darby said.

"You are going to fall. And"—he took a deep breath, which told Darby he was about to tell her the worst—"a hoof could hit you. I know a girl who almost got her brains kicked out falling down by the horse's hooves. And the horse wasn't even running. Hardly walking.

Come to that, you know her, too."

"Megan?" Darby asked.

Kit shook his head. "Little Samantha Forster and her Phantom, when he was a colt." Kit tugged the brim of his Stetson down as he added, "Boy, that was a tough time."

Darby thought of being kicked in the head. She knew how a hoof felt when she held it in her hands and balanced it on her knee for cleaning. Remembering the weight and hardness of it almost made her hesitate.

"This will be totally new to Hoku, and with her curious mind, I think it'll finish getting you two back together," Kit said.

That was all Darby needed to hear. She'd go along, but that didn't mean she wasn't scared. She swallowed hard and asked, "And Jonah said this was okay?"

Kit nodded. "Said he couldn't watch, though. That's why he's riding out to visit Tutu. Doesn't plan to come back 'til nightfall, after we're done."

Unless Kit calls Jonah's cell and tells him to come home fast and bring along Tutu, the next best thing to a doctor, Darby thought.

Darby acted on remote control, doing everything Kit told her to do, because he said working on one thing at a time was enough for the filly.

"Especially if she's had a whiff of Stonerow, she might be a bit, uh, restless around men."

Restless, Darby thought skeptically as she went into the broodmare pasture.

Kit had left the bag of carrots outside because he didn't want her to be mobbed by the other horses, but when Hoku saw her halter and lead rope, she came to investigate.

"So far, so good, beauty," Darby said as Hoku dipped her nose into the halter and kept her head lowered for Darby to buckle it.

Before she tried to lead the filly, Darby ran her hand over Hoku's back. She scratched a place that always seemed to be itchy and Hoku closed her eyes and stretched like a cat. Light as dandelion fluff, bits of what passed for a winter coat in Hawaii floated away.

"Let's go," Darby said, and headed toward the gate and the carrots, every bit as confident as if she was certain Hoku would follow. And she did.

"You know some of this already," Kit said as Darby led Hoku into the stallion's pasture. "Once you get all the gear on her, you're just going to jump up like you were going to ride bareback—"

"What about the war bridle?" Darby asked.

"We'll save that for the next time," Kit said. "Start with the halter, and sneakers. The hard-core warrior stuff can wait."

Kit was joking, but he was also rubbing the back of his neck and she'd come to realize that was something he did when he was nervous.

Together, they watched Hoku sniff around Luna's compound.

"Do you know how to do this?" Darby asked, finally.

"'Course. Me and my little brothers, all. We weren't no thirteen years old, either. We were doin' it while we were toddlers."

It sounded a lot like a dare, Darby thought. And Kit was lapsing into a thick Western accent he must think was funny. She'd give this a try and if anything went wrong, she'd protest that she'd done it just to shut him up.

Darby placed her hands on Hoku, letting her feel them, letting her know what would come next. Then Darby bounced on her toes and vaulted onto the filly's back.

"Take her 'round a couple times. Let her remember." Kit spoke in a normal tone though he was outside the fence, and Darby did what he said.

I love this, she thought as Hoku skipped from a walk into a swinging lope. Darby held the rope and mane, letting her legs hang close to Hoku's sides but not squeezing them. Soon Darby's body swayed in time with the filly's and she wondered how she'd come to be this girl who rode wild horses.

 Chapter Twelve

Darby only fell once.

She'd leaned farther to the right and farther, left hand burrowed as deep into Hoku's mane as she could get it. Lowering herself, holding the lead rope in her right hand, she rested her left heel on the leather band she'd tied around Hoku's middle.

It's not enough, she thought. The tiny bit of purchase the leather band offered her was nothing. It couldn't hold her body, but if she dug it in—

With an insulted neigh, Hoku's hind legs kicked out. Darby's left foot came loose and a blur of ground and grass rushed up to meet her right shoulder. Darby rolled, and came back up on her feet a little bit dizzy but fine.

She rotated her right shoulder. It felt all right, but she was giving it a rub when she caught movement along the fence. Kit had been running to help her, but now he stopped, hands on hips, and yelled, "Okay?"

She flashed a shaka, and walked over to Hoku. The filly had stopped just a few feet away, intent on sampling pasture grass.

"Again, baby," she told the horse.

Even though she hadn't been hurt by the fall, it took two more loping rounds of the pasture before Darby tried again.

"I won't fall this time," she told Hoku, "or you'll get the idea that falling is part of this trick."

Handful of mane.

Slip right.

Farther.

Don't look down.

Don't dig in left heel, just rest it there on that little leather ledge.

She stayed there a minute, halfway down, wondering what made Hoku keep going. Snorting and loping, ears pricked forward, the filly looked like she was having fun.

Darby's right knee clasped against Hoku, rising and falling naturally with the filly's gait. Then, Darby tucked her chin against Hoku's neck.

Hypnotized by the flow of movement and sounds, Darby clung to her horse, listening to Hoku's snort of enjoyment between every two hoofbeats.

Snort, strike, stamp, went her reaching front hooves.

Snort, touch, push, her back hooves propelled them, smooth and fast.

Darby would've had to inch forward and peer under the filly's neck if she had a bow to bend, a string to stretch, and an arrow to shoot, but she didn't.

She wished she could see her filly's face. Were her nostrils wide? Were her eyes half closed against the whipping of wind?

Hoku's heart beat steadily beneath Darby's cheek and she held on, right where she wanted to be.

Finally, Hoku's gait slowed and Darby pulled herself back up, astride her horse. She closed her hand more firmly around the lead rope and Hoku stopped whip-lash-quick.

"Good. We'll stop before she's exhausted," Kit said. "Much as she was likin' it, she would have run 'til dark."

Darby slid to the ground. She praised the filly and fed her carrots as she worked loose the knotted leather strip around Hoku's middle. Then Darby led her back to the broodmare pasture. As she slipped off Hoku's halter, the other horses crowded around, touching noses and sniffing Hoku for news.

Darby watched Hoku communicate with her pasturemates, then raise her head to follow Darby walking back to Kit. For the first time in weeks, Darby felt more confident. Hoku could find a place in the world of horses and the world of humans. At least, it looked possible.

As she fell into step beside Kit and they took the trail to Sun House, Darby said, "That was the most fun I've had in my life!"

"That strip around her middle is a lot like a cinch, so a saddle won't be such a surprise, even though she was concentrating on your contortions, and didn't really notice it."

"I'm starving," Darby said. For a few seconds her mind wandered to Megan and chopsticks, but when Kit stopped walking she asked, "What?"

"You know when you asked before, about Stone-row? He said some stuff about my grandpa Mac. My family don't tolerate that kinda disrespect."

It was almost dark and they'd finally sat down for dinner when Jonah came in, smelling of horse.

"You girls go get that filly—"

Darby stopped with a bite of tuna salad halfway to her mouth. "Hoku?"

"We got any other fillies that thieves are after?"

"Yes, Tango." Megan ventured the words carefully.

Jonah shook his head. "Bring 'em both up, put 'em in the round pen, and we'll set the dogs on watch."

Kimo offered to work through the night, saying he could always use a little extra pay.

He, Cade, Bart, and Sass would patrol the lower pastures. Peach would be locked in the ranch office behind a corrugated metal door Darby'd never seen closed. She figured locking the office was to prevent Stonerow from searching it, in case he returned to look for the adoption documents.

Jonah ordered Jack and Jill to guard the round pen. Adamantly, he muttered to them that no matter how Hoku fussed or traded defiant screams with Medusa, they were to *stay*.

It turned out Jonah was right. The three mares kept Darby awake for hours with their territorial calls. This *had* been Hoku's territory, and Tango's before that, but Medusa had declared herself the new queen.

As she listened, Darby's weary mind returned to worries of Shan Stonerow taking her horse.

The Nevada BLM hadn't called back, and Darby kept wondering what Sam would do in this situation.

Samantha Forster and her friend Jen—that was her name!—had tracked down details about Shan Stonerow's ownership of Hoku. They'd thought they were so important, they'd sent a fax, right after Darby had moved to Hawaii.

Darby rolled onto her stomach, pulled her pillow under her chin, and stared at her black headboard.

What if BLM didn't call back tomorrow morning? She had to talk to someone about this before Stonerow returned.

That meant Sam. And Brynna. Even if Brynna

no longer worked for BLM, she'd know their system. She'd know how this should be handled.

Darby knew she couldn't call. It was two o'clock in the morning in Nevada. But that didn't mean she couldn't send an e-mail.

Darby crept out of bed and tiptoed down the hall. Barefooted, she picked her way to the ranch office. Standing outside the door, she whispered, "Aloha, Peach."

She didn't want to surprise the dog into barking and waking up the entire ranch. Not that she believed anyone was sleeping through the mares' battle of vocal cords.

As Darby worked the door open, Peach gave a gentle woof. When she flicked on the light, he blinked sleepily, but didn't move from his curled-up spot on Aunty Cathy's chair.

"Aren't you cozy?" she asked. Peach sighed. "Hey, Peach, sorry, but I have to sit there to use the computer."

Peach yawned. He closed his eyes and laid his muzzle on his back, facing away from Darby.

"Okay, you can stay until I hook the computer up."

Darby crawled under the desk, disconnected the phone since the ranch only had a dial-up connection, and plugged in the Internet.

"Down," she said finally, and this time Peach believed her.

Darby tapped out an e-mail to Sam, telling her what was going on, and begging Sam to ask Brynna for advice. Then she changed her subject line from HI to PLEASE CALL IN MORNING—EARLY!

As soon as she logged out and closed down the Internet, she felt better. And so did Peach. He stood, stretched, and watched her expectantly.

"I won't tell if you won't."

Peach jumped into the chair and closed his eyes before she even left the office.

At last Darby knew she could sleep. She'd done all she could.

She walked back to her room in the darkness, rubbing her eyes and yawning. When she stopped and pulled her hand down, a dark figure materialized just ahead of her.

She gasped, even though it had to be Jonah.

"I'm sorry I woke you up," she whispered.

"No need to whisper. Who could sleep with those mares arguing?" He gave a disgusted grunt, but he didn't ask her where she'd been. His trust added another layer of comfort to her sleepiness. But then he said, "Darby Leilani?"

His voice didn't sound right, but she answered, "Yes? What's wrong?"

"Just this: Me and Luna were up on the ridge, watching you ride Hoku like a *pupule* paniolo girl and I have to say . . ." His voice trailed off.

Darby waited.

"Just, I wanted you to know—If I lose my sight tomorrow, it was worth it to see you ride that way."

Darby caught her breath. She flung herself at her grandfather, even as he said, "No, no, no. No sympathy." He complained as she hugged him around his neck. "Never should have told you. You're strangling me, girl. Now, go to bed."

Darby did, without a single word.

And when she got back into bed it turned out that she was just as tired as she thought. After this long outrageous day, she finally began to cry.

It was six o'clock when Darby woke up—nine o'clock in Nevada.

She stayed in bed reading for twenty minutes, but her attention wandered and, no matter how totally immature it was, she kicked her feet in impatience.

Magically, the phone began ringing. Darby jumped up, burst out of her room, careened around the corner into the kitchen, and snatched up the telephone.

"Hello?" Darby said.

"Take him to court," said a clipped female voice.

Darby wanted to laugh, but first she had to make sure she was talking to Sam's stepmother, Brynna.

"Mrs. Forster?" Darby asked.

"Of course, sorry." Brynna chuckled, and Darby could almost see her red hair and freckles. "This *is* Darby, right?"

"Yes, I guess Sam got my e-mail."

"She did and I've been thinking this over while I waited for a decent hour to phone. So, I think a judge's request will get Norman White—"

"The BLM guy?"

"Yes, my replacement, and though he's not managing things the way I did, he is a civil servant to his fingertips and judicial communication will get him moving in a hurry."

"Got it," Darby said, taking notes on the back of a power bill. "But do you think that Shan Stonerow could possibly have a case?"

"No. The paperwork you have is valid. There should be no problem."

Should, Darby thought. Why did she put it that way?

"But what about the freeze brand?" Darby asked.

"It's as simple as the filly's health. She was injured and traumatized. The freeze mark was low on our list of priorities. As much as I'd like to blame Norman White, that decision was mine. I advised letting the filly recover before she was branded. And Norman and I are both at fault for not confirming it had been done before she left the state," Brynna admitted.

"While you tie up Stonerow in small claims court, I'll write an affidavit, have it notarized and sent by overnight mail."

"Thank you so much," Darby said, taking notes as Brynna kept talking.

"Then, if the court doesn't just dismiss the case, I can film a statement for the courtroom."

The sound of a crying baby came over the phone

line and Darby remembered that Sam had become a big sister at Christmas.

"Sam said to tell you she e-mailed you," Brynna said, "and Cody says hi, too."

Darby smiled into the phone. Cody must be the baby.

"This helps a lot," Darby said, but Brynna rushed on.

"I promise to hurry and do this right away, and I e-mailed Norman White just before I phoned you and"—Darby heard the tap of computer keys before Brynna went on—"here's his response already. Darby, maybe you can get your grandfather or some . . ."

Darby waited, fingers crossed as Brynna's voice trailed off.

Aunty Cathy came into the kitchen, yawning. "I want oatmeal," she said. "It's cloudy outside—"

"And eighty degrees, Mom," Megan said, following her mother, then saw Darby on the telephone. "Who is it?"

"Nevada! I mean, it's Brynna Forster, the BLM lady and Sam's—hello. No! Really? Thank you so, so much! That is so cool. We'll get everything—no, he's already out, but Aunty Cathy's—here!" Darby shoved the telephone at Aunty Cathy. "It's Brynna Forster and she's coming over to deal with Shan Stonerow!"

"Throwdown in the 'Iolani corral," Megan crowed.

Aunty Cathy took the phone and bent over it, trying to block out the sound of Darby's celebration.

"Oh yeah!" Darby started to clap, but Megan grabbed her hands.

"Wait," she said, nodding at her mother, but Megan was laughing as she whispered. "She's coming here?"

"She got an e-mail from the BLM guy, and since BLM keeps no personnel in Hawaii and he couldn't get away on such short notice, he'd been on the phone with Washington, and they're flying her over as a special consultant, really soon."

"That's nice," Megan said.

"Not so much," Darby corrected her. "Apparently they're afraid of being linked to the commission of a felony. The thing is, Brynna can only stay for three days, so we have to get 'court proceedings' started without her, but I don't know anything about—"

Megan shushed her again and they both glanced over at Aunty Cathy. She was taking notes and squinting as if that would help her hear better.

"Of course you'll stay with us," Aunty Cathy was saying. "Unless you'd prefer a hotel? I know Darby would love to catch up with you, too."

Darby felt a wave of shyness. She barely knew Brynna Forster, but she had a lot to ask her. Hadn't Sam said her stepmother was a wildlife biologist? She'd probably fall in love with Crimson Vale, if there was time to take her riding there.

If only Brynna would bring Sam! Even if they only had two or three days, she and Megan could take Sam riding through the rain forest. Sam could meet

Tutu and see the ruined plantation. Or since beaches were rare in Nevada, maybe Sam would want to see the black sand at Night Digger Point Beach. Or Sky Mountain! She'd love Snowfire. He'd probably remind her of her Phantom. But, Two Sisters might be her first choice. Darby was pretty sure there weren't any active volcanoes in Nevada.

Her daydreams were disturbed by Megan's voice.

"I don't know how we can get Shan into court like the day after tomorrow," Megan mused. "We only have a justice of the peace, and this isn't exactly crime central of the Pacific."

"Are you talking to me?" Darby asked, and Megan half-pushed her out of the kitchen, past the bench and lined-up shoes, and into the ranch yard.

"Of course I'm talking to you! I'm so relieved. I couldn't stand it if you lost Hoku!"

Megan gave Darby a quick hug, then they began making as much of a plan as they could with the knowledge they'd gleaned from reading and TV court dramas. They were so involved in scheming, they didn't even notice Jonah's approach.

"What's all this?" he asked. "It's not bad enough I have three *pupule* mares screaming at each other all night? In the daytime I have girls blocking the doorway, clucking like hens?"

"You'll never guess who's coming to help us!" Darby said.

They were in the midst of explaining, and Jonah

looked relieved but a bit disgruntled at the unplanned-for houseguest, when the phone rang again.

The three of them entered the kitchen to see Aunty Cathy extending the phone toward Jonah.

"Kealoha," he identified himself sharply.

His eyebrows zoomed up as he listened.

"Who is it?" Megan hissed at her mother.

"Stonerow," Aunty Cathy whispered.

Darby wished they had a speakerphone for this conversation. But the next best thing was to watch Jonah for clues.

"Stonerow. Yeah, I could be interested in a civilized man-to-man talk. Depends." Jonah moved to the stove. "She's not my horse," he said, pouring himself some coffee that he must have made hours before. *"She's not my horse,"* he repeated, then glanced at Darby. "And my granddaughter's set on taking you to court."

Jonah smiled, then held the phone away from his ear, so Darby heard Stonerow's outburst.

"If you want to come over and look at her papers, it's fine with me," Jonah said. "I don't know what you mean by 'aggrieved' but if you've already filed with the court, maybe this will go faster. No, I wouldn't like to go to trial over a horse I already owned, but I tell you what I'd like less. Spending another night with these mares screaming at each other. And since I'm pretty worn out, I'm hanging up now."

And then he did.

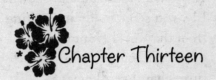

Chapter Thirteen

Before Brynna Forster was due to arrive, the BLM contacted the state attorney's office and arranged for an expedited trial. Brynna would be assisted by a local attorney named Sue-Jin Hart.

The attorney talked with Darby for an hour, gathering details she could follow up on. Afterward Aunty Cathy faxed her the adoption papers and Sue-Jin asked for Ellen Kealoha's phone number, because she was the legal owner.

"And you know, it wouldn't hurt if you faxed me that letter from your friend Sam about the history of your horse," said the attorney. "I might submit that."

When Brynna's flight was canceled and she was an entire day late, Sue-Jin called to assure Darby and

Aunty Cathy that it didn't matter.

"We have 'friends of the court' coming out of the woodwork," she said. "If Mr. Stonerow doesn't have character witnesses, he's going to be really unhappy. I've got Ed Potter, Brynna Olson-Forster, an affidavit from a Nevada tribal chairman named MacArthur Ely, and some really interesting records I subpoenaed from the Royal Hapuna Hotel."

"That sounds good," Darby said, but she wasn't sure what that all meant.

"Better than good," Sue-Jin said. "Once Brynna is here, we should be able to get your case together over lunch."

Darby had only met Sam's stepmother once, but when they got to the Hapuna Airport she immediately recognized the trim woman in a gray-green suit with her red hair in a tidy French braid as Brynna Forster.

What she didn't expect was her companion.

"Sam!" Darby rushed away from Aunty Cathy and past a security guard.

The Nevada cowgirl laughed as Darby almost knocked her off her feet.

"I didn't know you were coming! Oh my gosh, Hoku will be so glad to see you, well, at least I think she will. *I'm* so glad to see you!" Darby stopped and took a step back, a little amazed at the delight she felt at Sam's arrival.

While Aunty Cathy introduced herself to Brynna,

Sam tried to explain what had happened. She and her dad had been dropping Brynna off at the airport when her flight was canceled. The rescheduling was such a pain, they'd actually awarded Brynna an extra ticket to Hawaii. And since Sam's father, Wyatt, had no interest in leaving the ranch on such short notice and someone had to stay to mind Cody, Sam got to come along.

"But I didn't have time to pack or anything like that." Sam held her hands out in embarrassment. Sam wore jeans and a blue shirt over a dark blue tank top.

"You look fine," Aunty Cathy said and Darby agreed.

"All I had with me was this ratty purse, and even though we made two stops, every time we tried to dart into an airport gift shop, they'd call our flight! It was kind of funny, really," Sam said.

"Kind of insane," Brynna corrected. "And I might have just saved the ticket, but school's out and Sam has helped me with Cody every single day since Christmas. I thought she deserved a little break."

Sam's cheeks reddened and she shook her head as if helping with the baby was no big deal.

"I'm just so glad you're here. I have so many things to show you!" Darby exclaimed as they all walked out to the truck.

"I don't think I'm too much of a beach person," Sam said.

"That's okay. We're not really in that part of

Hawaii," Darby said. "It's ranch country, like Mrs. Allen's, only a lot greener!"

"Cool," Sam said, settling back in her seat, smiling.

"Although I bet you'd like riding on the beach, in the waves," Darby said.

"Now that sounds like heaven," Brynna said. "I'd like to try that someday."

"We can do anything you want tomorrow," Darby said. "The trial's not until Friday. I guess an attorney is coming over, but—"

"We're taking over the office for our meeting, but that doesn't mean you two can't go for a ride," Aunty Cathy said.

"And Megan," Darby said.

"Your almost-sister?" Sam clarified and Darby nodded.

"You'll love her. And, oh, you'll love Tango, her wild horse, too. She's a rose roan."

"I've never even heard of a rose roan," Sam said. "And I hope you'll still be happy to see me when I say I might have to borrow some of your clothes and wow, they might even fit. Darby, you look so different! Your breathing—"

"—is fine," Darby interrupted. "Everybody says it's the fresh air and exercise and, oh, you cut your hair."

Brynna reached over with short scrubbed fingernails to tousle her stepdaughter's reddish-brown hair. It was shorter, chopped off to chin length.

"Go ahead and say it," Sam laughed. "It looks like I hacked it off myself, and that's because I did." She slid her eyes sideways to glance at Brynna. "You should have seen it before Brynna trimmed it up for me. I sort of did it on a dare, and I'm already growing it out, but at least it will be cool for the summer!"

On the way back to the ranch, Darby told Sam all about training Hoku.

"And not a single buck?" Sam asked. "Even Ace keeps my attention with a little crowhop now and then."

"We'll go ride as soon as we get home," Darby insisted.

"It will be dark, Darby," Aunty Cathy said, "and these two have been flying all day. That takes a lot out of a person."

"I slept most of the way," Sam protested.

"But that doesn't mean the sun will stay up any longer." Brynna looked over her shoulder from the front seat.

"I know what we'll do," Darby said. And then she told Sam about Medusa and Kit.

"I hope he'll let us watch," Sam said.

"He will," Darby assured her. "He wants Medusa to make connections with other humans."

Sam nodded as if she understood. "That would be cool, and I can tell Jake all about it."

"And, listen to this." Quietly as she could, since she didn't think Aunty Cathy or Brynna needed to hear the details, Darby told Sam about Kit teaching her to "ride like an Indian."

"I wonder why Jake hasn't ever shown me how to do that," Sam mused.

"Maybe he doesn't know?" Darby suggested. "Isn't Kit years older?"

"Yeah," Sam said, considering, but then she said, "Never mind, I can guess."

Tilting her head close to Darby's, she told her about the accident Kit had mentioned.

"And Jake thought it was all his fault, even though it was all mine," Sam said.

"But not Blackie's?" Darby teased, using the name Sam had given the Phantom when they were both young.

"Of course not!" Sam said. "He's perfect."

". . . BLM said it was cheaper to fly me over and pay me as a special consultant than to fly the horse back to Nevada," Brynna was saying to Aunty Cathy. Then she glanced at the girls. "What are you two whispering about?"

"Nothing," they said together, but by the time they'd reached the ranch, Darby had promised to demonstrate riding like an Indian for Sam.

Sam rubbed her hands together as she listened.

"Jake Ely's going to get the surprise of his life," Sam said, and Darby had a feeling her friend couldn't wait to show Jake the stunt he'd neglected to teach her.

"You know, though," Sam added, "be careful, because it's possible it won't just hurt you, it could hurt Hoku."

Darby nodded solemnly.

That night, the adults were still sitting on the lanai talking when Darby and Sam slipped outside and headed for the bunkhouse. They couldn't wait to ask Kit if they could watch him work with Medusa.

"I'll walk partway with you," Megan volunteered. She and Sam had clicked just as naturally as Sam and Darby had. "I wish I could help, but there are four riders coming in tomorrow—two parents, a child, and a grandfather—and I'm in charge since Mom will be working with you guys and that attorney. So, I've got to get things organized now. But you know what? We should all go on the ride. It would be so much fun. And since you're a wild-horse expert, you could check out my horse, Tango."

"I'd love to see her, but I'm no expert," Sam said.

"That's not what I hear," Megan said. "Anyway, let's count on it. I'll even let you pick your own horse from the cremello herd."

"How could I say no?" Sam asked.

Bart bounced along beside Darby and Sam on their way to the bunkhouse. He clattered up the wooden steps and scratched on the door, so it was already opening when they arrived.

"Well, Samantha Forster! I am glad to see you again," Kit said, and Darby could tell he meant it, because he patted Sam on the back as hard as he would another cowboy.

"I hear you finally got your wild horse," Sam told him, and Kit nodded with a smile.

"This girl was with me and my brother at the Willow Springs Wild Horse Center in Nevada when I got that harebrained idea," Kit told Darby. "Guess I didn't lose it on my way across the Pacific Ocean."

"Are you working with Medusa tonight?" Darby asked.

"'Course," Kit said.

"Can we watch? We'll stay outside of the corral."

In the full minute Kit was quiet, Bart slipped past him into the house.

"Uppity dog," Kit muttered, looking after the Australian shepherd's fanning tail. Then Kit suggested, "Why don't you two grab helmets and help me inside the corral instead?"

"Cool," Sam said. "I'm up for it."

"Me too," Darby said.

"You want to run back up to Sun House and ask Mrs. Forster and Jonah first?" he suggested.

"They're busy," Darby said. Sam nodded.

"We'll have to be extra careful," Kit said. "Told you before: I don't want you costin' me my job."

"This is going to be so much fun," Sam said as they buckled on the helmets. "But hey, was there someone else inside the bunkhouse?"

"Cade," Darby said, nodding. "He's shy. But he's amazing with horses."

"Now where have I heard that description before . . . ," Sam said.

As they waited their turn with Medusa, Darby noticed Kit speaking quietly to the mare.

"That's not Hawaiian," Darby observed.

"It might be Shoshone," Sam said.

"You're right," Kit said in the same level tone he'd been using to his horse, "but I figure Medusa don't speak Hawaiian any more than she does Shoshone. And since the rhyme my grandfather gave me for sweet-talking animals is Shoshone," Kit said, shrugging, "what can it hurt?"

After what seemed like forever, Kit had haltered Medusa.

"She lets me do that, but not lead her," Kit said. "Maybe she'll walk along with one of you."

"I'll try it," Sam said.

"Me too," Darby agreed.

"Earlier today, me and Cade checked her mouth— wasn't that a rodeo!—to be sure there're no sharp edges on her teeth. That was the last thing I thought of that might make her resist leading—except fear."

"What if, since she was a lead mare, she doesn't want to follow?" Darby asked.

"Good idea," Sam said.

"You could be right," Kit agreed. "I thought maybe,

since she's in a strange place, she might not feel that way." Kit was quiet for a full minute. Then he asked, "Who's first?"

Sam held up her hand and Kit bowed her inside.

"Welcome to Hawaii," he said. "Now watch your head."

Both girls laughed, but Darby couldn't help remembering her first day in Hawaii. Kimo had taken her on a stomach-twisting exploration of Crimson Vale, and she'd been thinking *Welcome to Hawaii; excuse me while I throw up.*

"Here's what I think, Sam," Kit said. "If Medusa sits back against the rope, just stand up straight, drop your head, and relax. Then, I'll give my birdcall—"

"He sounds just like a meadowlark," Darby put in.

"And it won't feel threatening," Kit finished. "It's natural for her to startle and run from me, since I've been introducin' her to all this new stuff, but she has no reason to fear either of you."

It worked like magic.

For about thirty seconds, Medusa braced against the short lead rope, shaking her black mane, but then Kit gave his warble, liquid and sweet, and the mare followed Sam around the corral without question.

"I have chills," Sam said when Kit invited Darby into the corral to take over. "She's beautiful and amazing, and you've definitely been doing something right, Kit. I can't wait to tell Jake."

"If you'd seen her before," Darby said, "I mean,

just a couple nights ago, she was still rearing."

"My dad says that's the most dangerous vice a confined horse can have," Sam said.

"Wyatt's right," Kit said. Then he gestured for Darby to take the lead rope.

It didn't make sense, Darby thought, that Medusa acted practically tame for Sam and acted up with her, but maybe the humans' short conversation had given Medusa time to think. As soon as Darby stepped forward, the steeldust shied.

"Bug," Kit whispered, and Darby heard a chirring sound.

"You're okay," Darby told the mare, but at each tightening of the lead, Medusa reared instead of going forward.

Darby glimpsed Sam covering her mouth with both hands.

She's afraid for me, Darby thought, and even though Darby had no reason to prove anything to Sam, the girl who'd introduced her to wild horses, she wanted to show her how much she'd learned.

Determined, Darby took three steps and the mare did, too, but then she reared again.

Progress, Darby thought, and suddenly she realized what was wrong. Instead of thinking of Medusa, she was thinking of Sam and Kit watching her.

She relaxed her shoulders, took slow breaths, and let her eyes lose focus just a little bit. Then she began to walk, and felt a tiny pause before the mare's weight shifted to her back legs.

A horse can't buck if it's moving forward, Darby reminded herself. Without looking back, she sensed the moonlight spotlighting Medusa's muscles as they shifted beneath her silvery hide.

Thinking of a marching soldier, Darby let the lead rope snap tight between her and the horse and turned sharply left.

Medusa came along with a confused sniff, but when she tried shifting her weight again, Darby did exactly the same thing, except this time she turned sharply right.

Medusa followed, then stopped, studying her.

"Everybody out," Kit muttered. He opened the gate for Sam, then stood waiting. "Darby, see if you can get that halter off while she's still studying you, and we'll leave her with something to think over.

"You two did good," Kit said when they walked away a few minutes later. "Hoku'll be back in her home corral before you know it."

Only three guest riders showed up the next day, but it turned out Judge wasn't saddled in vain.

The parents were mounted on Maggie and Charisma, Darby swung into Navigator's saddle, Megan was ready to lead the ride on Tango, and Sam had chosen Makaha after Darby told her his last rider had been Stonerow.

"We'll just wipe that evil man out of your mind,"

Sam crooned to the white gelding, but then she followed the direction of her horse's ears down the road, to a puff of dust.

"You've got company," she said.

A blue van emerged from the haze.

"Are we expecting more Girl Scouts?" Darby asked Megan.

"I don't think so," Megan replied.

And then they saw the van stop short of the cattle guard and a figure climbed out.

"That's Pauli Akua, right?" Megan asked Darby.

"Your guess is as good as mine," Darby said, but she'd recognized him, too.

"A friend of yours?" Sam asked.

"Sort of," Darby said. "He hangs around with a guy we can't stand—"

"But I'm sure our guests aren't into high school gossip." Megan's forced smile warned Darby to be quiet.

"Absolutely," Darby said, and Sam nodded in understanding.

"Aloha," he called, jogging over. He tried to catch his breath and keep talking at the same time. ". . . favor for my mom. Know that girl who wore slippers the other day?"

Sam gave Darby a quizzical look and asked, "Bedroom slippers to go horseback riding?"

"No, flip-flops, you know, rubber sandals?" Darby explained the island expression, and Sam nodded.

"Another girl switched her for the extra sneakers in

her backpack," Pauli said, "but they were—"

"Go ahead and catch your breath," Megan told him.

"But I need to ride out with you and find it," Pauli said. He gazed at Judge and the bay lifted his head, sensing he might be going with the other horses after all. "And I wore boots." Pauli looked around for Jonah and Darby couldn't help smiling.

She didn't know how this guy rubbed off the taint of his friendship with Tyson, but he did.

"So, anyway, the sneakers were too mondo big for her and one fell off and she left it out there somewhere and didn't tell anyone until yesterday."

"I remember her," Megan said. "She told me her feet were hot and she'd just taken them off."

"Well, it turns out that the other girl, the one she borrowed them from, had stuffed her birthday money in the toe of the sneaker—"

"And we need to go find it," Sam finished.

Pauli looked at her thankfully, but confused.

"Samantha Forster, meet Pauli Akua," Megan introduced them. "Darby, why don't you help Pauli get on Judge and catch up with us in a minute? When we come back down from the ridge, we'll look for the shoe."

"Sounds good," Darby said.

Megan took the guests on, but Sam held Makaha back at the head of the trail.

"Thanks for waiting," Darby said, but her eyes

checked Pauli, making-sure he was settled in his saddle.

"You're welcome," Sam said.

"Hey, Judge, sorry," Pauli said softly to the horse. "I'm trying not to get all Quasimoto on you—" He straightened up when he saw Darby watching. "It's kind of hard to let go of this saddle horn thing."

"You'll get it," Darby said, then turned back to Sam.

"I wasn't really waiting for you," Sam confessed. "Just letting my eyes adjust to all of this green."

"This is the first time we're bringing guest riders up to Two Sisters pasture," Darby said.

"It's no place like home," Sam said, and her awe was clear.

"It *is* pretty," Darby agreed, "and there's a good view of the ranch."

"Where are you from?" Pauli asked.

"Nevada," Sam told him.

"What's with all these Nevada people?" Pauli blurted, then added, "No offense."

"Oh, wow, you haven't heard, have you?" Darby said, and she began telling him about Stonerow's claim. "The other day after you left, you know that jerk that was bullying Jewel?"

As they rode along, Darby told him the story. Sam added what she knew of Shan Stonerow's Nevada history as they followed Megan and the other riders up toward the Two Sisters pasture.

"That's weird," Pauli said, glancing back to the ground.

"What did you see?" Darby followed his gaze. Part of her job was picking up any kind of litter that might harm or frighten the horses.

"A book of matches from the Royal Hapuna Hotel," he said.

Darby backed Navigator and stared at it. Sure enough, the pink-and-purple square was decorated with a shaka-wielding gecko. She halted her horse and let the others ride on as she tried to puzzle out the significance of what she was seeing.

It was important, but why? Sure, she'd pick it up because it was gross to leave it out here. And yes, she'd seen the colors and logos at the Royal Hapuna Hotel. But there was more to it.

All at once, clues clicked together.

Shan Stonerow had stayed at the Royal Hapuna Hotel while he worked there. Shan Stonerow smoked cigarettes. And the ride she'd led that Stonerow had sneaked in was outside of the Two Sisters pasture. This proved Shan Stonerow had trespassed on 'Iolani Ranch property the other night!

"Yes!" Darby shouted. Still holding a rein, she slipped off Navigator and jogged back to the matchbook. "We've got him!"

"What's up?" Sam called. She wheeled Makaha back and brought him to a precise stop.

"Fingerprints! DNA!" Darby yelled. "Yahoo!"

"I don't know her very well," Pauli confided to Sam, in case the cowgirl thought Darby was crazy.

But Sam seemed to have caught on. "You think it's from Stonerow?"

"I know it is," Darby said as she nodded. "What should I use to pick it up with?" After looking around, Darby finally used her shirt hem.

"Do you really expect me to believe you'd never ridden before you got here?" Sam asked, grinning as Darby climbed one-handed into Navigator's saddle.

"If I were riding any other horse I couldn't do this. Thanks, boy."

Darby was too excited not to take the piece of evidence back to Brynna right away, but she wanted Sam to keep riding and fall in love with 'Iolani Ranch. And, with an expert like Sam along, it wouldn't matter that Megan was the only official guide. But Darby felt torn.

"I hate deserting you on your first ride, but don't you think I should go tell them?" Darby asked her friend.

"Go!" Sam said. "We'll catch up with Megan and get the tour." Sam pushed her reddish hair away from her eyes as if she longed to see even more of the rolling green land. "I wouldn't miss this for anything!"

Chapter Fourteen

Hapuna was a drowsy tourist town on weekdays, with little traffic.

Jonah pulled the horse trailer that carried Hoku into a shaded area next to the courthouse and Darby watched people walking between shops and office buildings. Many paused under palm trees planted around parklike swatches of grass. Some chatted beside raised marble flowerbeds and troughs filled with pattering fountains.

"She'll be okay here," Jonah said, checking the bolt on the horse trailer doors to make sure it was closed. "Don't imagine this will take too long."

Darby nodded. She was nervous, and more dressed up than she'd been since arriving in Hawaii. She wore a navy blue skirt, white blouse, and a silver clip held her hair back in a low ponytail. Even though it was a hot morning, and all the facts of this "case" were in favor of her keeping Hoku, Darby's hands were cold and shaking.

If I lose Hoku, my heart will break. Darby closed her eyes and thought prayerfully, *Please don't let that happen.*

"Your mom's plane should be here in ten minutes. The airport's so close, she could walk here. And you know she would, for you." Jonah patted her hand, then nodded for her to get out of the truck as more cars and trucks pulled up around them.

Her best friend, Ann Potter, arrived with her parents and their friend Patrick Zink. Aunty Cathy drove up with Kit, Brynna, and Sam. Sam broke away from the others. It was weird seeing someone else wearing her clothes, Darby thought.

Somehow Sam looked more grown-up in the short denim skirt and yellow blouse than she ever had, and she was coming this way on a mission.

"Cowgirl up," Sam said, and then pointed right at her.

"What?"

"Hoku needs you on her side. You can't look like the little mouse you were before you met her."

Darby caught her breath, then asked, "Are you trying to make me mad?"

"Is it working?" Sam asked, but she didn't smile.

"Kinda."

"Good." Sam gave her a hug and whispered, "You and the Phantom's little sis deserve each other. If the judge looks you over, she'd better see that."

"Okay," Darby said, staring after Sam as she darted back to Brynna, who was talking to a guard at the courthouse door.

Just before she reached the front steps, Sam shouted back at Darby, "Show 'em all!"

Then Cade arrived with Pauli Akua and his mother.

Those guys were keeping some kind of a secret, Darby thought. She had a feeling that it was something about Jewel, but Cade had refused to tell her until her troubles over Hoku were settled.

Darby recognized Richard from the Royal Hapuna Hotel. And a short, round woman in a pink suit was slipping out of a black BMW sports car and walking toward Darby.

"Aloha, Darby." The woman shook Darby's hand. "Sue-Jin Hart, attorney-at-law."

"Hi," Darby said. Up close, the woman was even tinier. Darby had never met an adult who'd made her feel like a giant. But that wasn't what worried Darby. She tried not to show her dismay. The state's high-powered attorney, the one that was supposed to take on evil Shan Stonerow, wore pink metal glasses with heart-shaped frames. Her briefcase was pink, too. She looked *cute*, not cutthroat.

The attorney introduced herself to everyone else, then walked inside, conferring with Brynna.

Darby's confidence nose-dived. Their case might be strong, but would the judge take Ms. Hart seriously?

Jonah obviously noticed.

"You ever seen one of those Venus flytrap flowers?" Jonah asked Darby as he nodded toward the courthouse.

"No," she said, wondering if this was really a good time for one of her grandfather's stories.

"They're all pretty and sweet on the outside, but full of sharp teeth where you can't see. That Ms. Hart, attorney-at-law, I think she's the same."

"I hope so," Darby said, but then Sam Forster's voice, telling her to *cowgirl up*, rang in her mind, and she told Jonah, "I'll be right back."

Darby ran back to their parking place. She touched her fingers to her lips, stretched her arm inside the horse trailer, and gave Hoku a kiss for luck.

Shan Stonerow sat alone on one side of the courtroom. A small stack of papers was centered on the table before him.

Darby realized a lifetime of watching television hadn't prepared her for the way a real courtroom was set up to intimidate you. The judge was seated high above everyone else. She was a big woman with a wide, placid face and she looked like she'd heard every excuse in the world. There was no jury.

"Ms. Hart, is the disputed animal available for inspection by a veterinarian?" the judge asked, once they'd gotten started.

"Of course, your honor, Hoku is just outside."

"Smokin' Kitty," Shan Stonerow corrected, but the judge gave no sign she'd heard him.

"Having viewed the DVD testimony from Norman White, and read through all relevant documents, including an affidavit from Katharine Sterling, to whom Mr. Stonerow once tried to sell his horse, and a fax from Samantha Ann Forster and Jennifer Kenworthy, all of Darton County, Nevada, I'm ready to make a ruling," the judge said.

What? So fast? Darby's heart pounded and the people around her rustled in surprise.

"Unless anyone present has something to add?"

"Do they ever, your honor," Ms. Hart said, and it didn't take long for Darby to see that Jonah had been right.

Despite her bubbly laugh and pinkness, Sue-Jin Hart *was* a Venus flytrap.

She introduced Mr. Ed Potter, who had known Shan Stonerow in Nevada.

"I don't think I was ever so mad at my dad as I was the day he sold a grulla colt of ours to Stonerow . . ." his testimony began, and Darby listened to the story of a horse Sam had told her about. His name was Jinx, and he was now a search-and-rescue horse, but not because

Shan Stonerow had trained him well.

As soon as Mr. Potter stepped down, with a glare, Stonerow thought it was his turn.

"Your honor," he said, "what about my bill of sale, photos, and the fact that this filly has no BLM freeze brand?"

The judge held up a finger meant to ask Stonerow for his patience, but then her gaze shifted to Darby. She sat up as straight as she could and tried to look like she deserved Hoku. As soon as the judge looked away, Darby shivered. Something in the judge's expression had worried her.

Next, Ms. Hart introduced Brynna Olson-Forster. She was just as businesslike as Mr. Potter had been emotional.

"Your honor," Brynna began, "all gathered wild horses are checked by a brand inspector, to make sure they're not stray or feral horses.

"The disputed animal, a female sorrel, approximately two years old, was injured on Rural Route 40. She had no brand and the filly's location was distant from Mr. Stonerow's home and from reservation lands where he is rumored to have released her.

"Besides a brand, the filly was searched for halter rubs, saddle scars, and other marks of domestication—"

"That's what I get for being nice! In the old days, we used to take a button or two off the end of the tail to mark our horses, but I liked that tail!" Shan railed.

Darby thought of Hoku's flowing, vanilla silk

tail. Of course it was beautiful, but what did it have to do with buttons? Was that a cowboy expression or Nevada slang?

Confused, Darby looked over at Kit. In a whisper, he explained that buttons were joints in a horse's tailbone and that sort of docking was done on some reservation horses. Darby started to reach for her own back, as if she felt the sting, the crack, and the cut.

Again the judge gestured for Stonerow to hush. Then she nodded for Brynna to continue.

"While the BLM admits the horse would customarily have been freeze-branded with a government number, the horse's frail health, temperament, and the long mane falling on the left side of the neck conspired to allow her to slip through without a brand."

Brynna paused, and added that she had come to Hawaii prepared to make the previous statement and to authenticate Darby's adoption certificate.

"However, since I've been on the island, I've discovered even more unsavory facts about Mr. Stonerow."

The judge didn't stop Brynna from rushing on, so she told the court how Stonerow had been hired by Royal Hapuna Hotel barn boss Christopher Mudge, a known horse thief. This had been discovered because Mudge had accidentally signed one page of his human resources paperwork with his alias, Karl Mannix.

"Your honor!" Stonerow interrupted again. "The government hired Mrs. Forster to cover up their mistake, not investigate me. I couldn't afford to bring my character witnesses to Hawaii."

"Don't be silly, Mr. Stonerow," Ms. Hart said. "Most of our testimony came via fax or the U.S. mail. That's certainly affordable."

"Objection, your honor." Shan looked smug, as if he'd finally recalled the right way to interrupt. "It's beside the point," Stonerow said, "all of this is because the animal's legal owner, Ellen Carter, isn't even here!"

"Sustained," the judge said. She folded her hands and looked at Darby.

Come on, Mom, come on! Silently, Darby begged her mother to hurry.

With an impatient rustle of black robes, the judge calmed Stonerow's outburst. Darby was just about to try to persuade the judge that the papers she had, saying the horse was legally adopted by Ellen Kealoha Carter, could be used in lieu of the presence of the owner, when Ms. Hart cupped her hand by her ear and Darby heard the sound of high heels clicking down the corridor.

Ellen swept into the courtroom.

"Your honor, please excuse me for being late."

"Mrs. Carter?" she asked, looking over the top of the glasses that had slid down her nose.

"Yes, ma'am," Ellen said, and then she took a seat just behind Darby and rested her hand on her daughter's shoulder.

Darby leaned her cheek over to rest on her mother's hand.

After the excitement that had flared up at her mother's entrance subsided, Darby still didn't like the look on the judge's face.

She cleared her throat and said she encouraged the two "owners" to negotiate and come to an agreement.

She sat back and looked between Shan Stonerow and Ellen. When neither spoke or even moved, she went on.

"If no agreement can be reached, since Stonerow can provide a bill of sale and photographs of the horse—"

No, Darby thought, *please no!*

". . . and if, in the opinion of a licensed veterinarian it is the same horse, Mr. Stonerow will be declared the legal owner."

"No!" Darby and her mother both jumped up and Jonah's fist hit the table.

"Your honor," Ms. Hart said in a weary tone, but the judge kept reading.

"However, since the legal owner abandoned his animal on public lands, BLM has advised me that said owner owes grazing fines amounting to a minimum of $3,752.27 and a maximum of $8,000.00. After said fees are paid, the horse must be transported back to Nevada tribal lands. There, the Department of the Interior, which includes BLM and the Bureau of Indian Affairs, may investigate Mr. Stonerow's charges that his horse was confiscated without cause. All fees will be covered by the animal's owner until such time as the government is deemed liable."

Darby tried to process what she'd just heard. It sounded like Shan Stonerow was going to have to pay an awful lot of money if he insisted Hoku was his lost Smokin' Kitty.

"That's blackmail!" Stonerow shouted, but then he collapsed into his chair and asked, "Can you repeat that, please?"

After the judge repeated the conditions of claiming Hoku, Stonerow relinquished ownership of the horse, made a slight bow in Darby's direction, and left.

What just happened? Darby wondered. Her mind spun until the judge left the courtroom. Then Darby was surrounded by hugs and laughter. Relief made her shed her short-sleeved jacket.

That's better, she thought. If only she could kick off her shoes, too. The heels on them weren't as high as those on her riding boots, but they felt closed-in and tight.

"I'm buying lunch," Ellen announced, and she led them off to a nearby sushi restaurant, recommended by Ms. Hart.

. Darby, Sam, Cade, Megan, Patrick, Ann, and Pauli sat at a table separate from the others and Darby tried to shake off the dazed feeling that kept her from believing her nightmare was really over. As they waited for their first course of sushi, Megan schooled everyone in the use of chopsticks.

Pauli sat on one side of Darby and Ann sat on the

other. Sam sat across from her, and it was the cow-girl's intentness on Pauli that made Darby notice his frown.

"What's up?" she asked him.

"You know that guy Mudge?" Pauli asked.

"Not really," Darby said.

"I know that guy *Mannix*," Sam cut in. "If that's his alias and he's the same guy, he looks like this innocent praying mantis—"

"That's him," Pauli agreed.

"He's so sleazy," Sam went on. "He stole some of our horses."

"Well, I didn't even know he worked with the horses, but he was in the hotel coffee shop all the time, where I work. One day, when I was getting chewed out for being late getting back from a break, he offered me a job. Said I could work for him on a container ship that ran back and forth between here and the main-land transporting livestock. I told him I was still in high school, and it seemed weird to him that I cared. But then I started wondering, back in the courtroom, do you think that's what Stonerow was going to do, when he was trespassing that first night, I mean?"

"Steal horses," Cade said as he turned away from his discussion with Megan. "And smuggle them onto a ship bound for—" He dropped his chopsticks.

"Let's go," Sam said suddenly. Everyone in the res-taurant looked at her, but she just jumped to her feet and grabbed Darby's arm to haul her up, too.

"What?" Darby asked, but she was standing, moving, letting the alarm in Sam's eyes spur her into action.

"Mannix," Sam began, but then shook her head as if even a few words would take too much time. "Brynna!" she shouted over her shoulder.

"What?" Darby demanded again, but she rushed past tables, down aisles, and out the door of the restaurant, instinctively heading for the horse trailer, for Hoku.

"That horse theft ring Mannix was in," Sam panted as she jogged beside Darby. "They stole horses from trailers a lot. Unattended horse—"

Darby kicked off her shoes and ran in her bare feet. She zigzagged between the fountains and planters, took a sole-burning shortcut through an asphalt parking lot, and dodged a man selling skewered pineapple from a cart.

Darby heard her friends behind her, and adults poured out of the restaurant, asking questions and following.

She heard the clunk of a metal latch. A horse trailer door slammed open. Hooves clattered on the street. And then she saw them.

A rope encircled Hoku's neck, pressing into the sorrel skin. Stonerow held the other end of the rope, but the one around Hoku's neck was tied with a slip-knot. It closed tighter.

"Where do you think you're taking her?" Megan's

soccer-field voice boomed out, alerting Stonerow that he'd been discovered.

Hoku's neigh was choked off by the noose just as Darby saw Sam point at a horse van across the street.

"Darby, don't!" Cade shouted.

"Wait!" Jonah yelled.

What do I have to be afraid of? Not Stonerow. He was trying to handle her defiant horse. She was only afraid Hoku would get away from him and fall.

Stonerow had prepared for losing. A horse van across the street, her mind repeated. *The street!*

"Get back!"

The voice was Pauli's but Cade was beside him. Both boys tackled Stonerow. Between them, Megan and Ann managed to flip the man onto his stomach. Then Patrick stuck the end of one crutch between Stonerow's shoulder blades and growled, "Don't move."

It all would have been great, Darby thought in despair, if Stonerow hadn't lost his grip on the lead rope.

Hoku saw her chance to flee. She scanned the area with wide, terrified eyes. Darby's arm was outstretched, and her fingers had almost reached the lead rope when the fire-gold filly leaped into a run.

Darby sprinted after her. So did Sam, Brynna, Kit—

All at once Darby knew what she had to do. She cut across the open space.

"Hoku, it's me, girl," she called as she scrabbled up onto one of the marble planters full of flowers. Then, as the filly veered wide-eyed in her direction, Darby leaped for Hoku's back.

Praying she hadn't miscalculated, that she wouldn't keep on going over Hoku's back, Darby touched mane and horse hide, and had the strength and balance to stay on.

The rope dangled between the filly's forelegs, lashing and tickling, changing Hoku's smooth run to an awkward, fractured gait. Darby couldn't stop looking at it. If she could reach the rope and use it for a rein, she could communicate with her horse, and maybe make her stop.

"Good g-g-irl," Darby managed. She wasn't stuttering or cold. The impact of concrete under hooves jarred every bone in her body and slammed her teeth together.

Darby heard raised voices. She saw speed-smeared faces and smelled fresh-cut grass.

Hoku was headed for a patch of lawn. It wasn't far off. She might have been able to stay astride if the pineapple vendor and that raised row of fountains hadn't been dead ahead. But they were and she had no choice. She had to grab that rope before Hoku ran out into the street, and she only knew one way to do that.

Handful of mane.

Slip right.

Farther.

Don't look down.

Don't dig in left heel, just rest it atop her back—where there was no leather strand!—then reach, reach . . .

Darby's fingertips touched the rope and grabbed it. Then she gave her trust to her horse, tucking her head against Hoku's neck and closing her eyes, as she held on.

A sweet fruity smell surrounded Darby in the instant before Hoku was airborne.

Water droplets sprinkled her legs as the filly stretched like a gazelle, and then they landed on the grass.

I'm still on, Darby thought.

Huffing and snorting, Hoku shook all over. Still, Darby didn't let go.

I made it. We made it.

Kit and Jonah reached them first, but Hoku screamed at the men to get back. She might have reared and then Darby knew she would fall, except suddenly, Sam was there.

Hoku went still. Darby opened her eyes and saw the Nevada girl with the reddish hair standing unafraid right in front of Hoku.

"Hey, pretty girl," Sam coaxed. "Know what I've got in this nasty little canvas purse? An oatmeal cookie from Nevada. I have a little filly of my own. Her name is Tempest. In fact, I think you're her aunt." Sam moved closer as she talked. "There's nothing Tempest likes better than my gram's oatmeal cookies. They're like sweet grain, smell? Only better." Sam crumbled off a bit of cookie.

Darby smelled cinnamon and nutmeg. She heard Hoku sniff. And though she tried to let herself down gently, Darby fell, still clutching the lead rope, onto the soft grass. She felt dizzy and lightheaded, so she didn't try to stand.

"Got her." Darby recognized Megan's voice and Ann's, from someplace nearby. Faraway, she might have heard Cade and Pauli shouting and saying something about officers and a brawl.

That got Darby back on her feet in time for her mother to grab her in a furious hug that nearly knocked her down again.

"I'm okay," Darby said, but, looking over her mother's shoulder, she saw that there really *were* police officers coming from the courthouse as Pauli said, "We have a radical citizen's arrest over here."

Ellen finally loosened her hug, but she kept her arm around Darby's shoulders.

"Wasn't Darby wonderful?" Sam asked Ellen as she tucked Hoku's lead rope into Darby's hand. "Can you believe she didn't know how to ride, just like six or eight months ago?" Then Sam whirled toward Brynna. "You know what we need to do?"

"What's that?" Brynna asked. She sounded cautious as she looked past Sam to Ellen.

"Darby could come work for us next summer in the HARP program!"

"Horse and Rider Protection," Brynna explained, mostly to Aunty Cathy and Ellen.

Aunty Cathy stood between Jonah and Megan, and Darby wasn't sure what to think. The three of them seemed to radiate every level of emotion known to human beings. Anger, fear, pride . . . love?

But Sam didn't notice. "It's a very cool program." She was trying to wheedle Ellen into nodding, but Darby only felt the arm around her shoulders tighten. "And I think Darby'd be a great role model for at-risk girls, don't you?"

Darby heard Ann's laughter at the same time she heard Brynna reply, "Honey, that's something we'll have to think about."

"Maybe she could practice a bit at our place," said Ramona Potter.

Around her, lots of people she loved were talking about her life, but when Ellen released her at last Darby only thought of Hoku. She edged closer to Hoku and rested her cheek on the filly's warm neck. Her horse was safe, and that was all that really mattered.

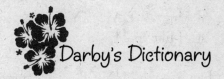 Darby's Dictionary

In case anybody reads this besides me, which it's too late to tell you not to do if you've gotten this far, I know this isn't a real dictionary. For one thing, it's not all correct, because I'm just adding things as I hear them. Besides, this dictionary is just to help me remember. Even though I'm pretty self-conscious about pronouncing Hawaiian words, it seems to me if I live here (and since I'm part Hawaiian), I should at least try to say things right.

ali'i — AH LEE EE — royalty, but it includes chiefs besides queens and kings and people like that

'aumakua — OW MA KOO AH — these are family guardians from ancient times. I think ancestors are supposed to come back and look out for their family members. Our 'aumakua are owls and Megan's is a sea turtle.

chicken skin — goose bumps

da kine — DAH KYNE — "that sort of thing" or "stuff like that"

hanai — HA NYE E — a foster or adopted child, like Cade is Jonah's, but I don't know if it's permanent

haole — HOW LEE — a foreigner, especially a white person. I get called that, or *hapa* (half) haole, even though I'm part Hawaiian.

hapa — HA PAW — half

hewa-hewa — HEE VAH HEE VAH — crazy

hiapo — HIGH AH PO — a firstborn child, like me, and it's apparently tradition for grandparents, if they feel like it, to just take *hiapo* to raise!

hoku — HO COO — star

holoholo — HOE LOW HOW LOW — a pleasure trip that could be a walk, a ride, a sail, etc.

<u>honu</u> — HO NEW — sea turtle

<u>ho'oponopono</u> — HOE POE NO POE NO — this is a problem-solving process. It's sort of cool, because it's a native Hawaiian way of talking out problems.

<u>'iolani</u> — EE OH LAWN EE — this is a hawk that brings messages from the gods, but Jonah has it painted on his trucks as an owl bursting through the clouds

<u>ipo</u> — EE POE — sweetheart, actually short for *ku'uipo*

<u>kanaka</u> — KAH NAW KAH — man

<u>kapu</u> — KAH POO — forbidden, a taboo

<u>keiki</u> — KAY KEY — really, when I first heard this, I thought it sounded like a little cake! I usually hear it meaning a kid, or a child, but Megan says it can mean a calf or colt or almost any kind of young thing.

<u>kupuna</u> — COO POO NAW — an ancestor, but it can mean a grandparent too

<u>lanai</u> — LAH NA E — this is like a balcony or veranda. Sun House's is more like a long balcony with a view of the pastures.

<u>lau hala</u> — LA OO HA LA — some kind of leaf in shades of brown, used to make paniolo hats like Cade's. I guess they're really expensive.

<u>lei</u> — LAY E — necklace of flowers. I thought they were pronounced LAY, but Hawaiians add another sound. I also thought leis were sappy touristy things, but getting one is a real honor, from the right people.

<u>lei niho palaoa</u> — LAY NEEHO PAH LAHOAH — necklace made for old-time Hawaiian royalty from braids of their own hair. It's totally *kapu*—forbidden— for anyone else to wear it.

<u>luna</u> — LOU NUH — a boss or top guy, like Jonah's stallion

<u>mahalo</u> — MAW HA LOW — thank you

<u>malihini</u> — MUH LEE HEE NEE — stranger or newcomer

<u>mana</u> — MAW NUH — this is a power you're born with. It's kind of a combination of instinct and intelligence.

<u>māna</u> — MAH NUH — I think to say this, you just hold the *ah* sound longer in your mouth and that makes sense. *Māna* means "knowledge you've gained

from the mouths of others."

<u>menehune</u> — MEN AY WHO NAY — little people

<u>ohia</u> — OH HE UH — a tree like the one next to Hoku's corral

<u>pali</u> — PAW LEE — cliffs

<u>paniolo</u> — PAW NEE OH LOW — cowboy or cow-girl

<u>papala</u> — PAW PAW LUH — cool fireworks plant!

<u>pau</u> — POW — finished, like Kimo is always asking, "You *pau*?" to see if I'm done working with Hoku or shoveling up after the horses

<u>Pele</u> — PAY LAY — the volcano goddess. Red is her color. She's destructive with fire, but creative because she molds lava into new land. She's easily offended if you mess with things sacred to her, like the ohia tree, lehua flowers, 'ohelo berries, and the wild horse herd on Two Sisters.

<u>poi</u> — rhymes with "boy" — mashed taro root with the consistency of peanut butter. It's such an ancient food, Jonah says you're supposed to assume the ancestors are there when you eat it.

<u>pueo</u> — POO AY OH — an owl, our family guardian. The very coolest thing is that one lives in the tree next to Hoku's corral.

<u>pupule</u> — POO POO LAY — crazy

<u>tutu</u> — TOO TOO — great-grandmother

<u>wahine</u> — WAH HE NEE — a lady (or women)

Darby's Diary

<u>Ellen Kealoha Carter</u>—my mom, and since she's responsible for me being in Hawaii, I'm putting her first. Also, I miss her. My mom is a beautiful and talented actress, but she hasn't had her big break yet. Her job in Tahiti might be it, which is sort of ironic because she's playing a Hawaiian for the first time and she swore she'd never return to Hawaii. And here I am. I get the feeling she had huge fights with her dad, Jonah, but she doesn't hate Hawaii.

<u>Cade</u>—fifteen or so, he's Jonah's adopted son. Jonah's been teaching him all about being a paniolo. I thought he was Hawaiian, but when he took off his hat he had blond hair—in a braid! Like old-time vaqueros—

weird! He doesn't go to school, just takes his classes by correspondence through the mail. He wears this poncho that's almost black it's such a dark green, and he blends in with the forest. Kind of creepy the way he just appears out there. Not counting Kit, Cade might be the best rider on the ranch.

Hoku kicked him in the chest. I wish she hadn't. He told me that his stepfather beat him all the time.

<u>Cathy Kato</u>—forty or so? She's the ranch manager and, really, the only one who seems to manage Jonah. She's Megan's mom and the widow of a paniolo, Ben. She has messy blond-brown hair to her chin, and she's a good cook, but she doesn't think so. It's like she's just pulling herself back together after Ben's death.

I get the feeling she used to do something with advertising or public relations on the mainland.

<u>Jonah Kaniela Kealoha</u>—my grandfather could fill this whole notebook. Basically, though, he's harsh/nice, serious/funny, full of legends and stories about magic, but real down-to-earth. He's amazing with horses, which is why they call him the Horse Charmer. He's not that tall, maybe 5'8", with black hair that's getting gray, and one of his fingers is still kinked where it was broken by a teacher because he spoke Hawaiian in class! I don't like his "don't touch the horses unless they're working for you" theory, but it totally works. I need to figure out why.

<u>Kimo</u>—he's so nice! I guess he's about twenty-five, Hawaiian, and he's just this sturdy, square, friendly guy. He drives in every morning from his house over by Crimson Vale, and even though he's late a lot, I've never seen anyone work so hard.

<u>Kit Ely</u>—the ranch foreman, the boss, next to Jonah. He's Sam's friend Jake's brother and a real buckaroo. He's about 5'10" with black hair. He's half Shoshone, but he could be mistaken for Hawaiian, if he wasn't always promising to whip up a batch of Nevada chili and stuff like that. And he wears a totally un-Hawaiian leather string with brown-streaked turquoise stones around his neck. He got to be foreman through his rodeo friend Pani (Ben's buddy). Kit's left wrist got pulverized in a rodeo fall. He's still amazing with horses, though.

<u>Cricket</u>—is Kit's girlfriend! Her hair's usually up in a messy bun and she wears glasses. She drives a ratty Jeep and said, to his face, "I'm nobody's girl, Ely." He just laughed. She works at the feed store and is an expert for the Animal Rescue Society in Hapuna.

<u>Megan Kato</u>—Cathy's fifteen-year-old daughter, a super athlete with long reddish-black hair. She's beautiful and popular and I doubt she'd be my friend if we just met at school. Maybe, though, because she's nice at heart. She half makes fun of Hawaiian legends, then

turns around and acts really serious about them. Her Hawaiian name is Mekana.

The Zinks—they live on the land next to Jonah. Their name doesn't sound Hawaiian, but that's all I know.

Wow, I met Patrick and now I know lots more about the Zinks. Like, the rain forest—the part where Tutu told me not to go—used to be part of the A-Z (Acosta and Zink!) sugar plantation and it had a village and factory and train tracks. But in 1890, when it was going strong, people didn't care that much about the environment, and they really wrecked it, so now Patrick's parents are trying to let the forest take it back over. They hope it will go back to the way it was before people got there. I still don't know his parents' names, but I think Patrick said his dad mostly fishes and his mom is writing a history of the old plantation.

Oh, and that part Tutu said about the old sugar plantation being kind of dangerous? It REALLY is!

Patrick Zink—is geeky, super-smart, and seriously accident-prone. He looks a little like Harry Potter would if he wore Band-Aids and Ace bandages and had skinned knees and elbows. He says he was born for adventure and knows all about the rain forest and loves Mistwalker, his horse. He's not into his family being rich, just feels like they have a lot to pay back to the island for what their family's old sugar cane plantation did to it environmentally. He likes it (and so do I!) that they're letting the rain forest reclaim it.

<u>Tutu</u>—my great-grandmother. She lives out in the rain forest like a medicine woman or something, and she looks like my mom will when she's old. She has a pet owl.

<u>Aunt Babe Borden</u>—Jonah's sister, so she's really my great-aunt. She owns half of the family land, which is divided by a border that runs between the Two Sisters. Aunt Babe and Jonah don't get along, and though she's fashionable and caters to rich people at her resort, she and her brother are identically stubborn. Aunt Babe pretends to be all business, but she loves her cremello horses and I think she likes having me and Hoku around.

<u>Duxelles Borden</u>—if you lined up all the people in Hawaii and asked me to pick out one NOT related to me, it would be Duxelles, but it turns out she's my cousin. Tall (I come up to her shoulders), strong, and with this metallic blond hair, she's popular despite being a bully. She lives with Aunt Babe while her mom travels with her dad, who's a world-class kayaker. About the only thing Duxelles and I have in common is we're both swimmers. Oh, and I gave her a nickname—Duckie.

<u>Potter family</u>—Ann, plus her two little brothers, Toby and Buck, their parents, Ramona and Ed, and lots of horses for their riding therapy program. I like them all. Sugarfoot scares me a little, though.

<u>Manny</u>—Cade's Hawaiian stepfather pretends to be a taro farmer in Crimson Vale, but he sells ancient artifacts from the caves, and takes shots at wild horses. When Cade was little, Manny used him to rob caves and beat him up whenever he felt like it.

<u>Dee</u>—Cade's mom. She's tall and strong-looking (with blond hair like his), but too weak to keep Manny from beating Cade. Her slogan must be "You don't know what it's like to be a single mom," because Cade repeats it every time he talks about her. My mom's single and she'd never let anyone break my jaw!

<u>Tyson</u>—this kid in my Ecology class who wears a hooded gray sweatshirt all the time, like he's hiding his identity and he should. He's a sarcastic bully. All he's really done to me personally is call me a haole crab (really rude) and warn me against saying anything bad about Pele. Like I would! But I've heard rumors that he mugs tourists when they go "off-limits." Really, he acts like HIS culture (anything Hawaiian) is off-limits to everyone but him.

<u>Shan Stonerow</u>—according to Sam Forster, he once

owned Hoku and his way of training horses was to "show them who's boss."

My teachers—

Mr. Silva—with his lab coat and long gray hair, he looks like he should teach wizardry instead of Ecology

Miss Day—my English and P.E. teacher. She is great, understanding, smart, and I have no idea how she tolerates team-teaching with Coach R.

Mrs. Martindale—my Creative Writing teacher is not as much of a witch as some people think.

Coach Roffmore—stocky with a gray crew cut, he was probably an athlete when he was young, but now he just has a rough attitude. Except to his star swimmer, my sweet cousin Duckie. I have him for Algebra and P.E., and he bugs me to be on the swim team.

❧ ANIMALS! ❧

Hoku—my wonderful sorrel filly! She's about two and a half years old, a full sister to the Phantom, and boy, does she show it! She's fierce (hates men) but smart, and a one-girl (ME!) horse for sure. She is definitely a herd girl, and when it comes to choosing between me and other horses, it's a real toss-up. Not that I blame her. She's run free for a long time, and I don't want to take away what makes her special.

She loves hay, but she's really HEAD-SHY due to Shan Stonerow's early "training," which, according to Sam, was beating her.

Hoku means "star." Her dam is Princess Kitty, but her sire is a mustang named Smoke and he's mustang all the way back to a "white renegade with murder in his eye" (Mrs. Allen).

Navigator—my riding horse is a big, heavy Quarter Horse that reminds me of a knight's charger. He has Three Bars breeding (that's a big deal), but when he picked me, Jonah let him keep me! He's black with rusty rings around his eyes and a rusty muzzle. (Even though he looks black, the proper description is brown, they tell me.) He can find his way home from any place on the island. He's sweet, but no pushover. Just when I think he's sort of a safety net for my beginning riding skills, he tests me.

Joker—Cade's Appaloosa gelding is gray splattered with black spots and has a black mane and tail. He climbs like a mountain goat and always looks like he's having a good time. I think he and Cade have a history; maybe Jonah took them in together?

Biscuit—buckskin gelding, one of Ben's horses, a dependable cow pony. Kit rides him a lot.

Hula Girl—chestnut cutter

Blue Ginger—blue roan mare with tan foal

Honolulu Lulu—bay mare

Tail Afire (Koko)—fudge-brown mare with silver mane and tail

Blue Moon—Blue Ginger's baby

Moonfire—Tail Afire's baby

Black Cat—Lady Wong's black foal

Luna Dancer—Hula Girl's bay baby

Honolulu Half Moon

Conch—grulla cow pony, gelding, needs work. Megan rides him sometimes.

Kona—big gray, Jonah's cow horse

Luna—beautiful, full-maned bay stallion is king of 'Iolani Ranch. He and Jonah seem to have a bond.

Lady Wong—dappled gray mare and Kona's dam. Her current foal is Black Cat.

Australian shepherds—pack of five: Bart, Jack, Jill, Peach, and Sass

<u>Pipsqueak/Pip</u>—little shaggy white dog that runs with the big dogs, belongs to Megan and Cathy

<u>Pigolo</u>—an orphan (piglet) from the storm

<u>Francie</u>—the fainting goat

<u>Tango</u>—Megan's once-wild rose roan mare. I think she and Hoku are going to be pals.

<u>Sugarfoot</u>—Ann Potter's horse is a beautiful Morab (half Morgan and half Arabian, she told me). He's a caramel-and-white paint with one white foot. He can't be used with "clients" at the Potters' because he's a chaser. Though Ann and her mother, Ramona, have pretty much schooled it out of him, he's still not quite trustworthy. If he ever chases me, I'm supposed to stand my ground, whoop, and holler. Hope I never have to do it!

<u>Flight</u>—this cremello mare belongs to Aunt Babe (she has a whole herd of cremellos) and nearly died of longing for her foal. She was a totally different horse—beautiful and spirited—once she got him back!

<u>Stormbird</u>—Flight's cream-colored (with a blush of palomino) foal with turquoise eyes has had an exciting life for a four-month-old. He's been shipwrecked, washed ashore, fended for himself, and rescued.

<u>Medusa</u>—Black Lava's lead mare—with the heart of a lion—just might be Kit's new horse.

<u>Black Lava</u>—stallion from Crimson Vale, and the wildest thing I've ever seen in my life! He just vibrates with it. He's always showing his teeth, flashing his eyes (one brown and one blue), rearing, and usually thorns and twigs are snarled in his mane and tail. He killed Kanaka Luna's sire and Jonah almost shot him for it. He gave him a second chance by cutting an X on the bottom of Black Lava's hoof wall, so he'd know if he came around again. Wouldn't you know he likes Hoku?

<u>Soda</u>—Ann's blue-black horse. Unlike Sugarfoot, he's a good therapy horse when he's had enough exercise.

<u>Buckin' Baxter</u>—blue roan in training as a cow horse and I can stay on him!

<u>Prettypaint</u>—used to be my mom's horse, but now she lives with Tutu. She's pale gray with bluish spots on her heels, and silky feathers on her fetlocks. She kneels for Tutu to get on and off, not like she's doing a trick, but as if she's carrying a queen.

<u>Mistwalker</u>—is Patrick's horse. She's a beautiful black-and-white paint—bred by Jonah! He could hardly stand to admit she was born on 'Iolani Ranch, which is silly. Her conformation is almost pure Quarter Horse

and you can see that beyond her coloring. And what he doesn't know about Mistwalker's grandfather (probably) won't hurt him!

<u>Honi</u>—Cade's mom's gray pony. Her name means "kiss" and she really does kiss. Cade jokes that his mom likes Honi best. He also says Honi is "half Arab and half Welsh and all bossy." And, she likes to eat water lilies!

<u>Snowfire</u>—an amazing mustang from Sky Mountain. He reminds me of Tutu's story about Moho, the god of steam—Pele's brother, too, I think—who could take the form of a powerful white stallion. Snowfire's conformation is like Black Lava's. He looks just as wild and primitive, and though they're about the same size, Snowfire just seems wiser.

❧ PLACES ❧

<u>Lehua High School</u>—the school Megan and I go to. School colors are red and gold.

<u>Crimson Vale</u>—it's an amazing and magical place, and once I learn my way around, I bet I'll love it. It's like a maze, though. Here's what I know: From town you can go through the valley or take the ridge road—valley has lily pads, waterfalls, wild horses, and rainbows. The ridge route (Pali?) has sweeping turns

that almost made me sick. There are black rock teeter-totter-looking things that are really ancient altars and a SUDDEN drop-off down to a white sand beach. Hawaiian royalty are supposedly buried in the cliffs.

<u>Moku Lio Hihiu</u>—Wild Horse Island, of course!

<u>Sky Mountain</u>—goes up to five thousand feet, sometimes snow-capped, sometimes called Mountain to the Sky by most of the older folks, and it's supposed to be the home of a white stallion named Snowfire.

<u>Two Sisters</u>—cone-shaped "mountains"—a borderline between them divides Babe's land from Jonah's, one of them is an active volcano.

<u>Sun House</u>—our family place. They call it plantation style, but it's like a sugar plantation, not a Southern mansion. It has an incredible lanai that overlooks pastures all the way to Mountain to the Sky and Two Sisters. Upstairs is this little apartment Jonah built for my mom, but she's never lived in it.

<u>Hapuna</u>—biggest town on island, has airport, flagpole, public and private schools, etc., palm trees, and coconut trees. It also has the Hapuna Animal Rescue barn.

<u>'Iolani Ranch</u>—our home ranch. 2,000 acres, the most beautiful place in the world.

<u>Pigtail Fault</u>—near the active volcano. It looks more like a steam vent to me, but I'm no expert. According to Cade, it got its name because a poor wild pig ended up head down in it and all you could see was his tail. Too sad!

<u>Sugar Sands Cove Resort</u>—Aunt Babe and her polo-player husband, Phillipe, own this resort on the island. It has sparkling white buildings and beaches and a four-star hotel. The most important thing to me is that Sugar Sands Cove Resort has the perfect water-schooling beach for me and Hoku.

<u>The Old Sugar Plantation</u>—Tutu says it's a dangerous place. Really, it's just the ruins of A-Z sugar plantation, half of which belonged to Patrick's family. Now it's mostly covered with moss and vines and ferns, but you can still see what used to be train tracks, some stone steps leading nowhere, a chimney, and rickety wooden structures that are hard to identify.

❧ ON THE RANCH, THERE ARE ❧
PASTURES WITH NAMES LIKE:

<u>Sugar Mill and Upper Sugar Mill</u>—for cattle

<u>Two Sisters</u>—for young horses, one- and two-year-olds they pretty much leave alone

<u>Flatland</u>—mares and foals

<u>Pearl Pasture</u>—borders the rain forest, mostly two- and three-year-olds in training

<u>Borderlands</u>—saddle herd and Luna's compound

I guess I should also add me . . .

<u>Darby Leilani Kealoha Carter</u>—I love horses more than anything, but books come in second. I'm thirteen, and one-quarter Hawaiian, with blue eyes and black hair down to about the middle of my back. On a good day, my hair is my best feature. I'm still kind of skinny, but I don't look as sickly as I did before I moved here. I think Hawaii's curing my asthma. Fingers crossed.

I have no idea what I did to land on Wild Horse Island, but I want to stay here forever.

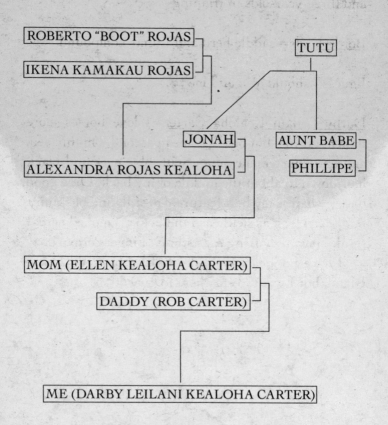

DARBY'S GENEALOGY

ROBERTO "BOOT" ROJAS

IKENA KAMAKAU ROJAS

TUTU

JONAH

ALEXANDRA ROJAS KEALOHA

AUNT BABE

PHILLIPE

MOM (ELLEN KEALOHA CARTER)

DADDY (ROB CARTER)

ME (DARBY LEILANI KEALOHA CARTER)

Don't miss the conclusion to Darby and Hoku's
Wild Horse Island adventures!

GALLOPING GOLD

*Galloping Gold

Sugarfoot had kind eyes.

Even though Darby Carter stood outside the pasture fence, she could see his eyes glimmer. When the gold and white pinto tilted his head, he looked sweet.

"Are you just totally misunderstood?" Darby called to the horse as she hefted a bucket and started to open the pasture gate.

"Careful when you go into the pinto pasture. Smudge and Red Cloud have manners, but you can never tell about Sugarfoot," cautioned Ann Potter, Darby's best friend. "He can fool anyone."

Including me, Darby thought. The horse didn't look a bit dangerous.

Sugarfoot grazed between a gray and white pony

and a rawboned mare, at least seventeen hands tall. Judging by the mare's drooping lower lip, she was old, but her bright bay and white coat gleamed like she'd just been groomed for a horse show.

Darby still didn't understand why Ann and her mother had been reluctant to ask her to keep Sugarfoot busy on the other side of the pasture while they had a visitor.

She made a kissing sound at the gelding and his ears pricked alert. If she hadn't known for weeks about Sugarfoot's habit of charging, she wouldn't have thought twice about spending time with the horse.

"Thanks for keeping an eye on Sugarfoot today. My mom just thinks it's safer for him to be watched when she's teaching someone who's never ridden before." Ann looked at Darby over the grape-soda-colored back of the horse she was saddling. "They'll be working in the arena and I'll just be standing over there for backup." Ann paused to retie the black ribbon headband that was supposed to tame her unruly red hair, and then glanced toward Sugarfoot again. "You're sure you don't mind?"

"Mind?" Darby asked. "Hmm, yeah, you know how I hate playing with horses."

"Just make sure he doesn't end up playing with *you*." Ann grinned as she settled a Western saddle onto Soda's back.

Darby couldn't take Ann's warning to heart. She'd been deprived of horses for the first thirteen years of her life. Now, she couldn't get enough of them.

Before, she'd lived in a world of fast traffic and crowded apartments. She'd only known the horses in books and her imagination.

Since she'd moved to Moku Lio Hihiu, the Island of Wild Horses, to live with her grandfather on 'Iolani Ranch, she spent every minute she could with them.

"Come on, Soda," Ann said to the blue-black gelding. She jogged forward, leading him by his neck rope. "Time to earn your daily grain."

For a minute, Darby watched them move away. Then she walked across the pasture toward Sugarfoot.

"And it's time for *me* to keep *you* out of trouble," Darby told the gelding. She swung the bucket of alfalfa cubes so the aroma would waft toward him.

Sugarfoot swished his tail with calm curiosity, but Darby caught something besides a craving for food in his expression as he lowered his head to the bucket.

Discover all the adventures on Wild Horse Island!